Westminster Press Books
by
ALICE MARGARET HUGGINS:

The Red Chair Waits

Day of the False Dragon

ALICE MARGARET HUGGINS

Author of "The Red Chair Waits"

Decorations by Jeanyee Wong

THE WESTMINSTER PRESS *Philadelphia*

Library of Congress Catalog Card No.: 53–6202

PRINTED IN THE UNITED STATES OF AMERICA

Day of the False Dragon

Chapter 1

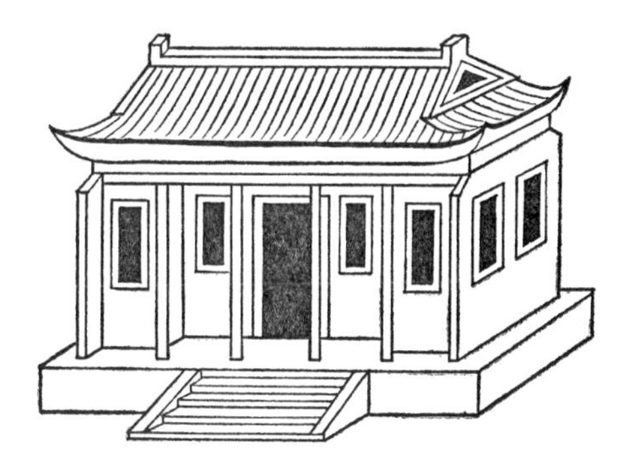

" Aren't you the teacher for the Girls' School? " Ling Ning heard a pleasant voice ask the moment she alighted from the bus at Wangshan.

" Yes," she answered the young man who had spoken. He was obviously an educated gentleman, though he was dressed in a faded gray-blue pajamalike uniform such as was being worn everywhere in North China since the Communist " Liberation " of Peking. " How did you guess? "

He gave a little jerk of his chin toward the shouting crowd around the bus and grinned. " I'm Lu Min. I was sent over by Principal Wang to meet the new teacher from Yenching University. Which one of these folks would you have picked? "

Ling Ning smiled back. She had already taken a liking to this young man with his frank look and easy poise. " I'm Ling Ning. You didn't even know my name, did you? The Yenching folks said they just telegraphed that they were sending someone on this bus, and left me to introduce myself."

" We're lucky to get you. When we lost our older science teacher two days before school was opening, you can imagine the shock! We asked Yenching to send us the best they could get, and are thankful they could secure so promptly one of their own graduates, and one they could recommend so highly."

"I hadn't quite made up my mind to teach school, but when I heard that the Christian girls' junior high school at Wangshan wanted a teacher for just what I'd majored in — I'd heard of Wangshan, you see, so I decided to come."

"And I hope you'll never be sorry. Now what about your baggage?" As soon as they had it collected, "Pirate's here to help with it," Lu Min said, with a turn of his wrist toward a sturdy workman with a wheelbarrow. To her inquiring look he answered: "He's one of the school men, and we call him Pirate, not to indicate his nature, but because that's really his surname. You'll find him one of the most useful citizens in Wangshan." He gave the man a friendly glance, showed him her box and bedding roll, and picked up her two small pieces. "I don't know how 'progressive' you are, but one Communist teaching which I accept readily is respect for work and willingness to do manual labor. I disagree with the old idea that a teacher must not carry anything heavier than a pen or a book. I'd like to be as helpful as Pirate."

Then he dropped his serious tone, and as they started along the street from the bus station, he smiled at her and said, "Well?"

"I feel as though I'd seen you before."

"Why not? I just graduated from Yenching myself last year. We're sure to have mutual friends, even though we don't know each other."

"Your name's Lu Min? Why, of course! I heard my roommate speak of you many times. You were both in the Christian Fellowship."

"That's right. When we have time to talk, we'll find we both know lots of others. But right now I ought to be showing you the sights."

They were following the crowd along a broad unpaved street toward a great city gate. On both sides were small shops, open to the street, exhibiting everything they contained. Many were full of vegetables or fruit. Apparently this was the center for buying food, because there were also occasional grain shops, and many small teahouses. The tables in front of these actually stood on the road, and the stools and rough wooden benches were crowded with men eating noodles, or porridge, or soup with a sort of salty doughnut.

Not all the crowd in the busy street were in motion. Children squatted in little groups here and there, playing in the dust with jackstones or marbles. Friends, having met unexpectedly, stopped and exchanged gossip. *Pai-t'ar-tis* — salesmen whose whole stock was carefully arranged on a piece of cloth a yard square, spread on the ground — were calling their wares: white pears, jujubes, crab apples, or whatever they had. Purchasers loitered along leisurely, stopping wherever they were interested.

On the right, outside the city gate, was a three-story, ivy-covered hospital, and here Lu Min turned east into a narrower, less crowded street. Taking for granted that Ling Ning had never been there before, he gave her bits of information about the mission hospital while they were passing it, about the big church they passed next, and then about the residence compound of the missionaries. "There aren't any Americans here now," Lu Min explained. "They all left when their Embassy asked them to. One, a Miss Graham, had been connected with our school for nearly thirty years. The others were doctors and nurses and church workers. We miss them, but, in view of what is happening in Korea, it's probably a good thing that they're gone. Their residences are occupied by Chinese." Through a gatehouse Ling Ning caught a glimpse of large gray-brick houses not unlike the faculty residences she was accustomed to at Yenching.

Lu Min paid no attention to the south side of the road. Along it ran high stucco walls with large black or red doorways at intervals. These were closed, but if one happened to be open, the "spirit wall" inside shut off all sight of the courtyard. They were entrances to comfortable Chinese residences such as the two teachers had seen all their lives.

"Do you know anybody here?" Lu Min asked.

"No." Ling Ning seemed to be about to say something more, and then to decide not to. "I know someone who used to live here," she finally added.

"It's a good enough place. Our Principal Wang is a prince — only thirty, young to be the principal of a girls' school. But he's really good. You'll like him. And I hope you find you like to teach. I do, immensely, though teaching isn't the simple job it used to be before the Liberation. We're to divide the science courses between us."

The two entered the Girls' School through a modest three-room gatehouse, and were in a neat, simple courtyard, surrounded by tile-roofed one-story buildings. The school was evidently entirely of Chinese architecture, a succession of courts like this. The buildings were all of gray brick, the upper half of each façade being clean paper windows, into which had been set small panes of glass. Along the front of each building ran a narrow covered portico with red-lacquered pillars. The brick end walls were softened and almost hidden by ivy. Everything was in good repair, and the brick pavement was swept clean.

The building facing the gate was larger than the others, and marked, "Assembly Hall." The two teachers turned to the right, where a long five-room building was labeled at one end, "Office," at the other, "Principal," and on the central door, "Teachers' Room." They entered this central door and found that the two offices at the ends connected with the larger central room, which was full of flat-topped desks set end to end to form a hollow square. Looking down upon them from the opposite wall were five huge pictures. Mao Tse-tung was in the center. On his left were Marx and Engels, and on his right, Stalin and Lenin.

Ling Ning's eyes widened. "They're bigger than the ones we have at Yenching," she murmured.

"We're more 'progressive' than you are at Yenching," Lu Min murmured back.

Through the open door into the principal's office they could see a young man and a younger woman working intently over a mass of papers on a big desk.

"She goes over all the principal's schedules and plans before they're announced," Lu Min said in a low voice.

Ling Ning got a good look at the two. They were dressed in the same faded, rumpled blue-cotton uniforms that Lu Min wore, except that the woman's had a Russian blouse with a belt instead of a loose jacket like the men's. She was large-boned and husky enough to be a farmer's wife. As she bent over her work, Ling Ning could see that her features were coarse and deeply pock-marked, and that she wore thick, shortsighted glasses.

Ling Ning was at once attracted to the slender, alert young man. Hearing them, he looked up, and immediately rose to greet her. His eyes were singularly sweet-tempered and friendly.

"Principal Wang, I've brought Miss Ling Ning from Yenching University," Lu Min said.

"And I welcome you in the name of the Wangshan

Girls' School," the principal said, bowing. He was one who would never be able to throw away his good manners, no matter how much the new age scoffed at old-fashioned courtesy. He turned to introduce his companion. "This is the politics teacher, Miss Pu, Miss Ling."

Ling Ning was surprised. Instead of the unprepossessing young woman she was looking at, she saw a bossing, heartless thirteen-year-old whom she used to fear when she was ten. "I — I think I ought to know you," she said hesitantly. Then, being stared at coldly by the other girl, she faltered, "Is your given name Fu-i?"

"It happens to be, but I'm sure I never saw you before," Miss Pu answered.

"Didn't — didn't you live in Peking — as a child?"

"Never! I've always lived in Harbin — till two years ago, when I entered the Revolutionary College. Now don't say I have a Peking accent! Of course I do. My family spoke Mandarin, and I had a Peking amah."

"It's just a coincidence, of course," Ling Ning said, trying to persuade herself that this was true. "There must be hundreds of little Chinese girls surnamed Pu, and sooner or later there'd surely be given names that were alike." She giggled nervously. "But you know how one is. When there's a similarity of names, one imagines there must be a relationship."

In spite of Ling Ning's conciliatory tone, there was an awkward pause and an odd tenseness. The principal changed the subject.

"We know how tired you are from that five-hour bus ride from Peking. School matters can wait until tomorrow morning, after you've had a good rest. Maybe Mr. Lu would be so good as to show you to your room and call the woman, and then he can consider his duty as welcoming committee done." He smiled pleasantly at Lu Min. "It's in the Big Court, Room Number — "

Miss Pu interrupted. "No. It's in the Side Court, that new little room. You know where," she said curtly to Lu Min.

"I thought we said — " the principal started to remonstrate. Then, with some embarrassment, he said to Lu Min, "You know where it is," bowed to Ling Ning, and prepared to continue his work.

Lu Min and Ling Ning walked in silence through groups of girls who stared at the new teacher. They stood here and there, or sat on the edge of the little porticoes. Most of them were dressed, not in bright colors such as had been fashionable when Ling Ning was a young girl, nor in the long blue gowns she had worn in high school and college, but in the new style introduced since the Liberation — short Russian blouses and loose trousers of dull cotton cloth.

The second court was similar to the first, but the buildings were classrooms. The third was dormitories. When he could do so without being overheard, Lu Min explained, "Being the politics teacher, Miss Pu — "

"Is the boss," Ling Ning finished for him. Such was not yet the case at Yenching, but she had heard how lower schools were being changed by the new politics teachers appointed by the People's Government.

"I was going to say that she doesn't have to be gracious to the rest of us." It was his apology for the recent rudeness of a fellow teacher to a stranger. "You don't have to be told how it is. But what I'm curious about is whether she was angry with the principal about something or whether she took a sudden dislike to you, or what. Because really your room was to have been Number Ten in the Big

Court. By the way, where did you think you'd seen her?"

Without the caution she had been learning to use since the Liberation, Ling Ning answered: "The girl I knew by that name looked just like this Miss Pu — pockmarks, shortsightedness, and all. My father bought her the first glasses she ever had. She was the daughter of one of our women servants and lived in one of our courtyards for several years, and, being three years older than I, used to be as mean to me as she dared without being found out. I could swear —"

"Oh, no. It's impossible. This Miss Pu is from a landlord family. She's told us all about her home life in Harbin. They apparently had oceans of money before the Communists took over. Her grandfather was put to death for his sins as a landlord, but her father, being an official somewhere in the south, ran off to Taiwan, and she no longer claims him."

"Her father was a ricksha puller, and he's been dead for years! I remember him well. He was my father's private ricksha man, a great big strong fellow, and when he died suddenly, my father took charge of the family, had them move into our place, and let the wife work for us to make a living. He paid tuition for the daughter at a primary school near us. I just can't believe it isn't she. There couldn't be two people so nearly alike with the same name."

They walked in silence a little way. Then Lu Min said quietly: "You can see that the beginning isn't very auspicious. I think you'd better disregard what you remember and start in here on the basis of what she has told us. Don't forget that, representing the Government as she does, she controls even the principal. She could make you a lot of trouble."

"You're right," Ling Ning agreed soberly. "Let's forget it." The advice was good. Work as a new teacher in this strange place might easily be hindered by an older girl in the powerful position of teacher of politics.

Through a narrow passage from one corner of a large dormitory court, they came into the Side Court. It was almost under the city wall, and seemed to be a sort of back yard, with small rooms, some of which were apparently occupied by servants, and others which were obviously storerooms and coal bins.

"Miss Pu didn't give you this little room as a compliment," Lu Min said, "but I'd rather have it than one in the Big Court. You'll find it much more quiet; when winter comes it will be warmer; the girls won't find it so convenient to come and rummage through your things; you'll get better service; and best of all — you see what a good salesman I'd make — do you see that small gate? It opens on an alley that runs behind the hospital to the main street into the city. I think it's a great convenience to be able to go and come without having every student out in front know when and where. I know, you see, because the dormitories of the men teachers are right there." He pointed to the wall of an adjoining courtyard. "And we have a gate out, just like this. What's more," he said, as he opened the door into the room, "it's just been done over — fresh window paper, fresh whitewash on the walls, and I happen to know everything has been given a dose of DDT, so you won't have bedbugs. It's a pretty nice room." The little room was really pleasant enough, and Lu Min's effort to make her see its good points was successful.

"I think I'll like it," Ling Ning was saying as a fat old woman appeared.

"Here you are, Granny Mi!" Lu Min exclaimed, and introduced the new teacher. "And now my part is done as soon as I direct Pirate with your baggage. The two of them will help you get settled. I'll see you at the faculty supper table."

Ling Ning had hardly finished thanking him when Pirate appeared with the bedding roll and box. He and Granny Mi were friendly, as well as efficient, and Ling Ning, who was used to servants, knew how to direct them and get acquainted at the same time. They had both worked at the school for many years and knew everybody and all the ways of the place.

When they finished, Granny Mi said in her matter-of-fact, cheerful voice: "Just rest your heart! I'll be in the next room. I heard Mr. Lu cheering you by telling you what a nice place you have. You'll find he's right. You'll be better off than in the Big Court."

Ling Ning was tired, but thinking of her mother at home alone except for two old servants, she took pen and paper and wrote her a long letter. The encounter with Pu Fu-i had recalled vividly their family life as it had been in those days before the Japanese invasion. Then not only her father had been living, but her grandfather too — officials, both of them, and scholars, with wealth they had been born to, and lands off in the country in addition to their residence in the East City, a house that was really an old palace. Ling Ning wondered whether Pu Fu-i knew of the changes that had come in that home since she had left with her mother ten or more years ago. During the Japanese occupation of North China, Ling Ning's father died, and then the old grandfather, bereaved by the loss of his only son, followed him, and left only Ling Ning and her mother. With the establishment of the Communist Government, they lost all their lands. Then to pay the taxes, and to give her daughter the best education she could secure, Ling Ning's mother sold one courtyard of the home after another, and rented out yet other courts. The two of them were not really poor even now, in spite of all the changes. They had kept three courtyards and two old servants. And if they should lose those, there was always her mother's family to fall back on — five loyal brothers, all well-to-do, the sons of another old Peking official family. In their childhood the sister had been tutored with her brothers until she was the equal of any of them in the old-style learning, and even now she continued to be their equal in knowledge of current politics and news.

Ling Ning was comforted by writing to her mother. She could picture her mother's beautiful patrician face as she read with eager interest. The two of them enjoyed each other unaffectedly, as good friends do, and no compliment ever gave Ling Ning so much pleasure as when someone told her, as someone often did, that she was growing more and more like her mother.

It was well that Ling Ning used her first free evening for her long letter home. She found the next few days full of "meetings." The faculty members were assigned desks in the "teachers' room" and, during the days while the students were busy with registration, met there constantly. The most insignificant questions were discussed endlessly. Everyone must express an opinion, and when all had spoken, Miss Pu would settle the matter. She said very little, but nothing was decided against her wishes. Ling Ning had never been a teacher before. She was wearied by all the matters that must be attended to before she could even begin to teach — deciding upon the sponsors for the classes, the advisers for the wall newspaper, the auditors for the girls' kitchen committee, the schedules for leading assembly, for explaining the news from the newspaper, and for assisting with all sorts of student activities, many of them quite different from the ones she had engaged in as a high school girl. In these matters Ling Ning had no opinion, but was called on each time to express one. She recognized this as good Communist procedure, but with aching head she wished that since Miss Pu always decided the question in the end, she might do so in the beginning, without all the palaver. If the others felt restive, they concealed it, and the business droned on.

The meetings had one great advantage for Ling Ning. She saw all her colleagues and heard them talk until she not only knew their names and voices, but had some idea of the temper of each. After a while it occurred to her that this was one reason for so much discussion — to let all see what each thought — and that she was giving herself away with every comment. They would know whether her "point of view" was "right." Remembering Lu Min's murmured comment, "We're more 'progressive' than you are at Yenching," she tried to speak very carefully, and to appear as "progressive" as she could. She must not let anyone get the idea that she was reactionary.

The teachers' desks had been assigned by subjects. Lu Min's was beside the door into the school office. Ling Ning, being the other science teacher, had the next one. On her other side was the physical training teacher, Mr. Chen. Opposite them, under the pictures of Marx and Engels, were the mathematics teachers, then geography, history, and politics. That put Pu Fu-i in the opposite corner of the room from her. The rest of the desks belonged to the teachers of Chinese language and literature.

While the meetings were going on, Lu Min on one side of her and Mr. Chen on the other frequently scribbled on pads on their desks and passed her bits of information. She was the only new teacher. The others were almost all men, and most of them seemed to have been with the school for many years. During the six weeks' summer vacation there had been a summer school, where the teachers had lived together and spent long hours of concentrated study on "politics" under the tutelage of the Government educational department. Occasional references to the summer discussions revealed how difficult it was for these adults, who had always enjoyed a great deal of freedom, to attain the required uniformity in their thoughts. Ling Ning suspected hidden friction, and could see plainly a self-conscious formality toward Miss Pu which often became a bid for her favor. Ling Ning was not the only one who was trying to sound as "progressive" as possible. They were all doing it. The principal, as chairman, was unfailingly pleasant and courteous. At no time was there any outward expression of disharmony, but Ling Ning was sure that the apparently perfect accord was a sham, as false as if they were acting in a play.

Sitting directly across from her was a most attractive young man, Mr. Yang, one of the mathematics teachers. He was tall and handsome, with a strong, low voice. She noticed him at once, at her first morning meeting, but took pains not to look at him because he kept watching her. At noon he walked with her to the dining room. Knowing she came from Yenching University, he tried to discover some mutual acquaintances, but the names he mentioned were only names she had heard, not people whom she knew.

"What's your university?" she asked.

"I'm Fu Jen, two years ago."

"Are you a Catholic, then?"

"No, I don't have any religion."

" I supposed when I came here that the teachers in a mission school would all be Christians, though I'm not one myself."

" That would have been nearer true a few years ago," Mr. Yang told her. " These older men are all Christians, and the principal too, but none of us who have come since the Liberation have any connection with the Church. Pu, and Chang who sits next to her, are actively antagonistic. The two of them are determined to blot Christianity out of this school, which has had a reputation for being unusually religious. Now that the American woman has gone on furlough, Lu Min is the one they are after. The other teachers are docile and stay away from church, but Lu Min goes to the services and makes it no secret that he's as good a Christian as ever."

" Why shouldn't he? " Ling Ning asked. " The Government has guaranteed religious liberty."

" That's what he says. You just wait. They'll get him into trouble for something else, and his religion will be the real reason. Only I'd better be careful what I say to a stranger! " he laughed.

Ling Ning changed the subject by asking whether Mr. Yang knew certain acquaintances of hers at Fu Jen. They were still talking about this when they were joined by some of the other teachers at the door of the dining room. There were only eight teachers, since most of the faculty had homes nearby. They ate fast and conversed little while they ate. Having finished, Mr. Yang again accompanied Ling Ning as she went back toward her room. At Yenching she had been used to walking and talking with young men and working with them quite naturally. Now she was surprised to find how self-conscious Mr. Yang's attentions made her. They had to walk through courtyards full of girls, who stopped everything to watch, and Ling Ning felt her face hot with blushes. Peeking at Mr. Yang, she discovered that he had noticed her embarrassment and was amused by it. This added to her discomfiture. At the end of each courtyard she tried to give him a chance to leave her, but he always managed to be in the middle of a question, or to be waiting attentively for an answer. And so they came to the Side Court.

"How did you happen to get stuck in this little spot?" he asked.

"Oh, I prefer this," she said, talking faster than usual. "I'm afraid that if I had a larger room I'd have to share it with another teacher, and I'm used to being alone at home. Besides, if I were in the Big Court, I'd have to be responsible for keeping order among the girls, and I don't want to have to do that."

"Keep order among the girls! You're years behind the times. You're thinking about when you were a high school girl. Nowadays you wouldn't dare tell them what to do. Don't you know they're liberated?" Then, mimicking a student's shrill young voice, he sang out: "Liberated! Truly liberated!" It was a good imitation. And Ling Ning heard a chuckle from Granny Mi's room next door.

Mr. Yang laughed. "Pu put you here, not the principal. She had some reason. Not knowing any more about it than I do, I'd make the guess that it made her pretty sick to see such a good-looking girl come here to teach, so she put you as far out of sight as she could."

Ling Ning made a modest objection to the compliment, but was interrupted.

"Don't you have a mirror? Even so, for Pu to put you out here is rather extreme. You didn't make her mad or anything, did you?"

Ling Ning had a momentary impulse to tell him what she had told Lu Min about Miss Pu's childhood. For all he was so friendly and seemed unafraid of Miss Pu, she thought better of it. " I'd rather be here," she repeated. " It's more convenient in every way."

" As you say, being away from the center has its advantages, but I hope it's not an indication that Pu's got it in for you."

Ling Ning unlocked her door and entered, prepared to say good-by for the present. But Mr. Yang followed her in, and cheerfully seated himself when she sat down at her desk. She was not used to having a strange young man in her room. This one required no entertaining. He almost immediately noticed a pile of music on the corner of her desk.

" What? Do you play? "

" Some. I've had enough lessons so that I ought to be a lot better than I am. Even though I'm not very good, I enjoy the piano, and Mother likes to have me play for her."

" Duets! " he exclaimed, turning the music over. " I can play a little too. Let's go! " He was picking up the music.

" No," Ling Ning stopped him. " Not right now. It's only a little while till the next meeting, and if you don't mind I'd like to rest till then. You must remember that this is all new to me, and I get tired."

He was instantly sympathetic. " Surely. Any time will do for the music."

" After supper then, when one wants a little relaxation. Where do we play? "

" In the assembly room. You know where it is, up front. This is going to be a treat."

At the evening meal Mr. Yang talked about music with such enthusiasm that when they had eaten and he and

Ling Ning were starting to the assembly hall, their colleagues followed, and the first practice was attended by an audience. Ling Ning had brought all her music, but wisely chose the book of easiest duets, playing the upper part herself. Mr. Yang's ability was hardly sufficient for what he had to play, but he had a good sense of rhythm and found enough of the notes so that he was delighted with the performance.

Ling Ning looked around after the first piece and discovered that the assembly hall was half full of students who, hearing the piano, had come running to see what was going on. The duets were simple old songs, and soon Mr. Yang was singing with the piano. He had a good baritone voice, so when they finished that piece, Ling Ning found a book of songs and played for him "The Last Rose of Summer" and "Auld Lang Syne." These were received with applause from the now augmented audience, and they went on with their impromptu concert until the warning bell rang for the evening "meeting."

"This is wonderful!" Mr. Yang enthused. "We're going to have fun."

Ling Ning had enjoyed it herself more than she would have believed possible. Neither of them noticed that not one bit of the music was of the new Communist era. They had played and sung from her old books, and it was all pre-Liberation or even American in origin.

On one of the first days after Ling Ning's arrival, a clerk came from the tailor's shop where the other teachers had bought their uniforms and measured her for an outfit with a Russian blouse like Miss Pu's. He promised the uniform in two days, and delivered it promptly. Ling Ning washed and packed away in her box the clothes she had been wearing. The new ones had not a single element of beauty, but at least she looked as though she belonged here, and did not advertise by her clothes that she was a new teacher.

Now only her hair was out of style. In June, to be bridesmaid at a classmate's wedding, she had got a permanent like all the other members of the wedding party. In Peking there were plenty of girls with permanent waves. Besides, all her life she had worn what she pleased without self-consciousness. Here she was conspicuous, the only one with curled hair among the hundreds of straight bobbed heads around her. In this small place everybody knew everybody else and noticed all deviations from accepted behavior. In addition there was a new feeling. The group had the right to control the individual in everything, great or small. The girls openly pointed at her hair and made comments she could not fail to hear.

One of the slogans the students shouted was: "Liberated! Truly liberated." Truly liberated indeed! Ling Ning had never before in all her life felt so restricted.

Chapter 2

Ling Ning knew she was fortunate to have the desk next to Lu Min, for this permitted her to ask about the school's customary procedures. She found that she was more fortunate than she had at first thought. When they compared their class schedules, they found that they had in common a vacant period the first thing in the morning, and that the only other teachers who were free at that hour were at the other end of the room and did not include Miss Pu or her satellite, Mr. Chang. It was not that Miss Pu paid any attention to Ling Ning. On the contrary, for the most part she acted as though she did not see her. But Ling Ning was uncomfortable in her presence, and relaxed at the thought of enjoying a vacant period when she would not be under Miss Pu's eye.

"This is nice!" Lu Min exclaimed on the first of such mornings.

"I hope you continue to think so," Ling Ning confessed. "I'm going to ask you questions all the time."

"I'd already planned to find time to help you a lot if you want me to. I haven't forgotten how hard I found my first month. I'm teaching what I taught last year, and I'll have both my records and my experience to fall back on. So my work will be light."

“It’s really good of you!” Ling Ning said, and meant it with all her heart.

“Having all the physics and chemistry gives you all the girls in the second and third years,” he said.

“And having all the first-year sections for hygiene once a week means I teach everybody in school,” she finished.

“I couldn’t see why Miss Pu insisted on that. I think it’s hard for a new teacher. But you’ll soon get used to it, and you’ll know them all in a few weeks.”

He showed her how to make charts of the seating in the two upper classes so that she could find in the classroom any girl whose name she had, and know the name of any girl seated before her. He promised to make her copies of the seating in the first-year sections, before she should meet any of these classes. He explained the lesson plans which must be filled out at once for the Government education department, and went to the school office and found those of the preceding year and gave them to her as a model. He gave her some ideas for her first sessions with the older girls, all of whom he had taught the year before. The first hour of his tutelage gave her a confidence that carried her easily through the rest of the day.

The schedule was a strenuous one. The rising bell rang at six. At six thirty pupils and teachers had ten minutes of exhausting physical exercise together, and then separated to their various rooms for an hour. The students prepared their lessons, but for the teachers this hour was given to the study of some Government-issued pamphlet or magazine on a subject selected by the educational department: politics, economics, educational methods, some subject in which they wished the teachers to change their thinking to the Communist point of view. It was an hour of intense group study, led by the principal. Then came breakfast.

At eight thirty, everyone stood at attention in the front courtyard during the raising of the flag and the singing of "*Chi lai.*" After that came the schedule of classes. Evenings brought the teachers another period of study from seven to nine, the subject again being assigned and the material sent out by the Government educational bureau.

Ling Ning liked best those days when part of the "study" consisted of listening to a lecture on the radio. There was no danger of her being suddenly asked a question when she had let her mind wander. Sometimes she paid no attention at all to the radio, but just relaxed. If it had not been for Lu Min's daily help, she would have found the first weeks beyond her strength.

She had been made sponsor to the C section of the first-year class — fifty-five little girls as strange to their surroundings as she was. She could only announce to them that they might come to her if they thought of any way she could help them, and then hope that somewhere in the crowded day there would be time to attend to their wants.

The first week had not passed before she was called on at her bedroom before supper by two girls whose faces were not yet familiar. They were both crying, but the older one managed to stop.

"Our name is Wang. I'm not in the class you're sponsor for, but my little sister is. We're in trouble and don't know where to go, and she says to come to you."

Ling Ning smiled to reassure her and urged her to go on.

"The girls call me 'Tientsin,' and everybody calls her," she pointed with her chin, "'Little Sister.' I'm in the third-year class, and I've had aid ever since I came here two years ago. And we thought it was all fixed up for Little Sister to come here with free tuition too. But now we've been told that both of us have to pay. You see, we're Christians, and this term no Christians are on the aid list, but only girls in the Youth League."

So the Youth League was involved! The members were Miss Pu's special pets and, being "children of the Communist Party," had so much prestige and power that the very name was mentioned with awe.

"Miss Pu's my class sponsor, but it wouldn't do any good to go to her. She's the one who took away our scholarships. And the tuition has to be paid before day after tomorrow or we have to go home. I just can't leave! I want so badly to finish this school." She burst into sobs.

Ling Ning finally quieted her enough to ask what sum was needed.

"If we each pay half the tuition on time, we can pay the other half later," Tientsin explained.

"How much is it?"

"The tuition is four measures of corn apiece, so we'd have to have four measures to divide between us."

"In money?"

"Four *wan*."

Ling Ning had brought twenty *wan* with her as spending money until she should receive her first month's salary. She had paid for her uniform. She could spare four *wan* and solve the immediate problem for these two distressed children.

Tientsin, watching her, guessed her impulse. "My father couldn't possibly get it here in time. I don't even know where he can borrow the other half later, but if you'll only give us this now, we'll not ask you again."

"Will you promise not to tell anybody where you got it? Let them think a classmate lent it to you?"

Upon their promise, she gave it to them quickly and hurried them away from her room, hoping that no one had seen them there. But a few minutes later, when Granny Mi came in, Ling Ning was sure of at least one person who knew what she had done.

"She's a nice girl, that Tientsin," Granny Mi began, "and never spends an extra copper. Her folks are good Christians in Tientsin. She goes to church here, even now that Miss Pu tells them not to. The girls all say Miss Pu is going to drive the Christians out of the school or make them back out of the church. You see, I'm interested because I'm a church member myself, but of course I can't attend services on Sunday morning — not nowadays."

Ling Ning knew she must not discuss Miss Pu with one of the school servants. "Probably," she said, "I shouldn't have helped the children without asking somebody, but it wasn't a very large sum. Only please don't tell anybody about it."

"You'll find I don't gossip," Granny Mi assured her. "I'd have lost my job years ago if I had. But sometimes," she cackled gaily, "I listen to some!"

Ling Ning did not mention the affair to Lu Min, though by keeping their voices low and their heads bent over their desks, they could carry on confidential conversations with the assurance that not even someone passing to or from the office would notice. She told him a great many things, but on the matter of the loan she kept her own counsel.

School had opened the third week of August. Now in early September the weather was beautiful — cool in the mornings and evenings and clear and sunny at noonday. Not more than five miles north of Wangshan were low mountains. Ling Ning, looking toward them from the narrowness of the Side Court, wished for time to go outside and get a better view. There were classes five and a half days a week, and even Saturday afternoons and Sundays had been filled with assigned work or meetings or even extra classes.

But on one Saturday morning Lu Min announced: "We're going on a picnic tomorrow afternoon. I've asked the principal and he says the afternoon's free. I have two very good friends I want you to meet, and this will be an opportunity."

"Wonderful!" Ling Ning exclaimed. "Where are you going?"

"We haven't decided yet, but we can get four bicycles and take a real trip."

"Oh — could we — "

"What?"

"Go to the Temple of the Blue Lake? It must be six or seven miles from here, on one of the nearest hills."

"Surely! But how do you happen to know about the Temple of the Blue Lake?"

Ling Ning was red with confusion. "I'll have to confess to you, but I'd rather you didn't tell anybody else."

He promised.

"I spent the summer here the year before the Liberation. My mother's oldest brother was the Wangshan official, and she and I visited his family. That's why I was interested in coming here to teach. But you see he was a Kuomintang man — "

"So that actually he would have been a good reason for staying as far away as possible from here! Does Miss Pu know about him?"

"I don't suppose she would remember the name of my mother's family. It's Wang — so common that if she remembered the recent county official was named Wang, she'd have no reason to connect him with me."

"But with the Government pushing its drive against reactionary elements in society, any connection at all with the old Kuomintang is dangerous. You are probably not conscious of how dangerous. Haven't you been reading in the newspapers about the execution of former Kuomintang officials, for no other sin than their former positions? Why, sometimes the whole family is taken into custody."

"I know, and it is frightening. But I don't think anybody suspects me of being connected with him, or knows I was ever before in Wangshan."

"We must neither of us mention it to anybody — to anybody at all — not even to the good friends who go with us tomorrow."

"Tell me about these friends," Ling Ning urged.

"Well, the three of us are a sort of little Christian group — like a Communist cell. They're Timmy Tan, over at the Rural Service Center, and Nurse Sun. He studied agriculture in America and she's a graduate of P.U.M.C., and I suspect they'll get married eventually. So sometimes I feel a little left out when we go off on one of our picnics. Having noticed that you look as though you'd been working too hard, I suggested that we take you along, since they both want to get acquainted with you."

Anticipation of the excursion brightened the day, and preparations took the extra minutes. The next day at one o'clock, Ling Ning pushed Pirate's bicycle through the little back gate Lu Min had promised her would be useful, and joined him in the alley that ran toward the hospital.

Ling Ning felt at home at once with Nurse Sun, thanks to their similar Peking and Yenching background. The other girl, perhaps five years older, was instantly congenial. As for Timmy Tan, Ling Ning found him charming, and suspected that he had depth of character which she would know only on longer acquaintance. They also wore the common gray-blue uniform, but Nurse Sun's head was tied in a gay flowered kerchief and she carried a handsome purse. Timmy Tan's good leather shoes and Leica camera differentiated him from the common crowd.

The day was perfect. They were released from burdens of responsibility and fear of criticism. Every remark was full of gaiety as they pedaled toward the beautiful hills rising ahead. Ling Ning knew her muscles would be sore on the morrow, but because of the daily morning exercises she was not too flabby. They fairly flew over the well-built auto road, on which there was considerable traffic — automobiles, farm carts and donkeys, rickshas, cyclists and pedestrians. The crops on both sides of the road were a rich green: millet, with its heavy yellowing heads; tall kaoliang, with beans beneath; corn; sesame; castor beans; sunflowers; and occasionally some plant Ling Ning did not recognize. The harvest would be plentiful.

Naturally there was very little conversation on the way, beyond gleeful calls back and forth. When they reached the first big hill, they alighted and pushed their wheels ten or fifteen minutes until they came into full view of the Temple of the Blue Lake. Here they stopped with exclamations of admiration.

The temple had been built on the hill in deep terraces, court rising above court. The first terrace, outside the entrance hall, was laid out with a long avenue between old white-barked pines set so far apart that they framed, but did not interfere with, the vista which rose in seven great steps, the topmost building clear-cut against the sky. From among the trees the rosy walls and green-tiled roofs glowed richly in the brilliant sunshine. Bells hanging from under the corners of the roofs tinkled softly in the distance, being caught by breezes not felt at the foot of the hill.

“It’s a lot like the Purple Cloud Temple west of Peking,” Nurse Sun commented.

“I think it’s more impressive,” Ling Ning said. “It’s much more beautiful than the Summer Palace and a lot of the other places tourists used to visit year after year. And to think it’s off here at Wangshan where nobody has known anything about it.”

“Probably it wasn’t built to make an impression on tourists,” Lu Min remarked, dryly.

They approached slowly, enjoying its beauty, and stopped while Timmy Tan took a picture. The nearer they came, the more the stateliness of the entrance building impressed them. Just outside it to the right was a food seller’s stand, with rough tables and stools. The food seller was a wrinkled old fellow, with head either bald or so closely shaven as to appear bald. But he was brisk and businesslike, and the four of them had soon arranged to leave their bicycles with him while they climbed to the top of the temple.

Not until she saw the signs in the gatehouse did Ling Ning realize that the buildings would not be as she remembered them. The Government had long since taken over all the temples for other uses. Here the signs gave directions for finding the various Governmental organizations which now filled the great courtyards: the local primary school, the Women’s Union, the Communist Party headquarters, the health department, the police, the Cooperative Society headquarters, the propaganda department, the Society for Friendship with the Soviet Union, the young people’s league, the Pioneers, and so on. The list was as long as the numerous local activities of the new Government. Inside of a little window a young man seemed to be acting as information officer, telephone boy, and general manager. He assured them they might go where they pleased. "This place belongs to the masses!" he intoned. "Extraordinary liberty!"

Ling Ning's enthusiasm was slightly deflated by the changes. She had thought she was coming to a place of peace and age-old quiet. To her companions, who had never been here before, nothing was lacking, and she joined with them in appreciating the beauties they pointed out. Everything was well cared for, and it was clearly a busy place, being used to serve the neighborhood much more effectively than it ever was as a temple. She expressed this idea to Lu Min, and found that he had little regret for the loss of the temple. The other two had wandered away.

"Religion ought to be such an essential part of life that it could not be removed," he said. "If this temple had offered such a religious expression to the people of this neighborhood, I think they could have kept it as a temple, or at least part of it, even though the Communist Party has no religion."

They climbed up and up, stopping on each terrace to look out across the plain to the walls and gates of the little city of Wangshan, set in green farm lands.

It was only upon reaching the top terrace that they could see the other mountains beside and behind this one, and below, in the nearest valley, the tiny Blue Lake. Here they rested a while and talked quietly. The problems and weariness of the last few weeks seemed far away.

Sometime later they started down slowly, stopping and going into side courts whenever a view seemed attractive. Sometimes these side courts were just groves of pines, or had in them a little *ting-za,* where in former times a monk could find solitude. Sometimes they were gardens full of cabbages or sweet potatoes. It was a huge place, and it was no wonder that they failed to meet Nurse Sun and Timmy Tan. On each level only a glance was sufficient to show that all the main buildings were used for meetings or offices. None were crowded, but people came and went, intent on their own affairs. And in no place was there any sign that for centuries worship had been carried on there.

Outside the gatehouse, the little food stand was deserted except for the old food seller, sitting on a stool behind his counter.

"We'll have some tea now," Lu Min ordered, "and something to eat when our friends come."

The old man brought the tea and cups. After a surreptitious quick scrutiny, he asked Ling Ning, "Haven't you been here before?"

"Oh, no! . . . That is, yes — I was here once when it was a temple, before the Liberation."

"With Official Wang and his family, and a beautiful lady, your mother?" the old man added.

Ling Ning was startled. "Yes, but how did you know?"

"I was the abbot here then," he answered. "Official Wang was a good friend of mine, and I remember that visit clearly."

"The abbot!" Ling Ning could recall the abbot and this man did indeed look like him, now that she was searching for a resemblance. "But the abbot! To be selling tea!"

"All the priests have gone into some occupation where they can make a living. This was my only home for so long that I hated to leave it. I make a living here and enjoy the beauty, and have time for contemplation too. Business isn't so good as to make me too busy for that."

Now she could see that his face was not without the wisdom and dignity she remembered in the abbot of the Temple of the Blue Lake.

" And you? What are you doing here? " he asked.

Ling Ning told him about her present circumstances and introduced Lu Min.

" What about your uncle, Official Wang? "

" He's living quietly in Peking. He's over sixty and thinks of himself as retired. You know his hobby has always been calligraphy. He spends some time at that, and reads. He's not rich, but he has enough. I think the People's Government wanted him to take training and continue to work, but he says it's the young people's turn."

" He was the best official Wangshan County ever had," the old man said. " He was a Christian, and most of the others were good Buddhists, but he really cared about the people. Look at the roads he built, and the schools! The one he started here in our first court had over two hundred pupils. And he talked every temple in his district into giving up enough room for a primary school."

" I've heard him tell about his schools," Ling Ning smiled. " He thought there was no excuse for keeping education for the well-to-do and the city people. I don't think Chairman Mao himself can be any more enthusiastic for schools for the people than my uncle."

" And the roads! Did you notice the one you came out on? He built them in every direction from Wangshan City to the edge of his county, and then bought a car and rode on them himself. He used to say that if there were good roads the people would find better means of transportation. They'd use buses and trucks instead of riding donkeys and pushing wheelbarrows. And before he left there were bus lines all over the county."

" We came out here in his car that time."

" He toured around and knew what was going on, and that little car of his helped him save the time to do it. Of course there was grumbling about the taxes. The Kuomintang taxes were heavy. But you can't make me believe he put any money into his own pocket."

"He didn't need to," Ling Ning interposed. "The family had quite a little."

"That's not the reason officials do it," the abbot replied. "What money he didn't turn in, but used locally, was a farseeing investment for the people. He was a really good official." The former abbot sighed, and then went on in a hoarse whisper, though there was no one near. "He has an enemy in here, named Wu." He jerked his head in the direction of the temple. "I knew the fellow when he was an underofficial. Your uncle jailed him for bribery. Then when Wangshan was liberated and all the prisoners freed, Wu became the most hothearted progressive of them all. He hasn't forgiven your uncle. I heard him lecturing one day. He declared Official Wang had built all the roads in this county with the public taxes, but for his private enjoyment, so he could ride around in his car and look down on the people. He cursed your uncle terribly for exploiting the people to fill his own purse. I thought he got a little confused and introduced some of his own sins."

Nurse Sun and Timmy Tan appeared in the gateway. "I'd rather not talk about him before these friends," Ling Ning interrupted the abbot, though she was anxious to hear all he could tell her about her uncle. "It's all right before Mr. Lu here. He knows about my uncle."

"Official Wang ought to know what Wu is saying," the abbot whispered anxiously. "He's dangerous, especially with the Government hunting for an excuse to execute former Kuomintang men. Can't you give him a hint?"

Ling Ning nodded, but there was no opportunity for further conversation. The abbot became the busy food seller. He offered a choice of millet porridge or cabbage soup, and when they chose the latter, he took a wooden cover off a small iron caldron and ladled out big steaming bowls of the savory mixture. They bought sesame cakes to eat with it.

Long before dark the four friends were back in front of the hospital. " I wish you could come in a while," Nurse Sun said to Ling Ning. " I've hardly talked to you at all." She made a little face at Timmy Tan, who laughed.

" She can," Lu Min offered. " It's three quarters of an hour yet till evening study. We've had our supper. I'll take Pirate's wheel back, and tell Granny Mi to be ready to open the back gate in about thirty minutes."

Ling Ning visited Nurse Sun's room, met one or two other nurses, and chatted more freely than she had at any time since she had come to Wangshan.

" My, how fast I've jabbered! " she exclaimed when the half hour was over. " I guess I've missed having other girls to talk to more than I knew. Miss Pu is about the only other girl teacher over there."

" And I know Miss Pu! " Nurse Sun laughed. " I'd think it was awful if you didn't prefer me to her. Now you know the way, you must come over often. I mean every day. It's near enough."

" Yes, it's near enough, but I don't know when you're free."

" Oh, that's easy. I get through at five every afternoon, and I wish I had someone interesting to talk to."

The time was just right for Ling Ning, and accepting the invitation she began the very next day to slip out the little back gate from the Side Court and spend a half hour with Nurse Sun before supper. Granny Mi knew where she was, but she was away so short a time that there was never any necessity to call her.

Chapter 3

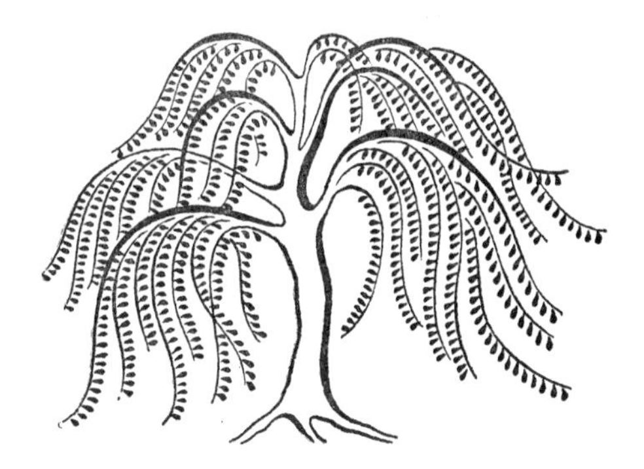

At the end of each month each "small group" held a "criticism meeting," writing down what was said and sending the minutes up to the next larger division. This division sent them on to a still larger division until the reports reached the principal, who put them into better form and turned them in to the local Government educational department.

Though it had almost twenty members, the faculty had never been divided. It counted as a "small group." There were those who guessed the reason: Miss Pu could not divide herself and attend more than one group, and could not content herself to hear only half of what was said.

So after four weeks of school Principal Wang announced at Saturday morning study hour that instead of the regular schedule the teachers should meet all morning with the classes they sponsored to help the students. At one o'clock they should come to the teachers' room prepared for criticisms of themselves and each other, the meeting to continue as long as was necessary. Afterward Principal Wang warned Ling Ning that every new teacher was expected at her first criticism meeting to give an autobiography. To make a good first impression, the principal advised Ling Ning to put at least part of it in writing unless she felt herself a competent speaker.

Ling Ning had taken part in many criticism meetings, both as a student at Yenching since the Liberation and, somewhat less comfortably, during the month of intensive political training that had been given all that year's university graduates during the summer. Then she had been only one of a large body of students who were learning the techniques of living in a Communist society. Now she was a teacher and the Government was making it very clear that the thoughts and attitudes of teachers were of the utmost importance.

What she said today would be read carefully by the local educational department and kept on file. " Self-criticism " was always difficult. Today's was formidable.

Lu Min had little to offer beyond the advice, " Drag it out as long as possible and sound as progressive as you can," and the assurance that she had his sympathy.

In every moment she could steal from the morning she wrote notes of what she must remember to say and missed lunch to put her thoughts into better order. When the bell rang at one, she was nearly ill with tenseness and apprehension.

As she entered the room she did not notice Mr. Yang standing just inside the door until he said in her ear, " Don't be frightened, little girl."

" *Mei ch'u hsi!* Good-for-nothing! " she answered rudely, being startled. Then, seeing his grin, she added, " I'll try not to, most venerable sir."

Perhaps the principal knew that being the first to speak would be hard for her, and that waiting too long would be almost as difficult. Perhaps he guessed where there was likely to be conflict and thought he might as well have it over. Or possibly it was mere accident that made him say, upon opening the meeting, "We'll begin with Lu Min and just go round the circle," indicating by a wave of the hand that the direction put Ling Ning second.

Her thoughts were concentrated on herself, but she must learn all she could from Lu Min's performance too, so she listened attentively how he began with disparaging remarks about his shameful lack of development in political consciousness, in spite of so many opportunities and the constant wise leadership of Chairman Mao. He went on to say that, though he knew it was important, he had found the recent study of economics less interesting than other subjects, and he promised to try to increase his liking for that field, which was so essential in a Communist society. He mentioned some problems he had met in sponsoring his class, problems he claimed would be solvable as soon as his point of view was more correct. He had written out all he had to say and, upon finishing, handed his paper to the principal.

Ling Ning began to tremble, and her lips moved in what she had planned was to be her first sentence. But the principal did not call on her, and she soon noticed that the teachers were not looking at her, but at Lu Min. Now that he had finished, it was time for the others to criticize him. Finally one spoke and then another, commenting on his self-criticism or making suggestions about the problems he had mentioned. The men who spoke did so in a friendly tone and there were long pauses between comments, so much so that Principal Wang would ask, "Who will speak?"

In one such pause with Ling Ning expecting any moment to hear her name called, Miss Pu said: "I hope Mr. Lu will set as one of his goals the renunciation of his superstitions. Then our school can have its science teachers really scientific in their point of view."

At her words all in the room stiffened to attention and Lu Min himself sat up with a jerk. "Will you explain what superstition you mean?" he asked.

"The Christian myth," said Miss Pu.

"That's my religion."

She shrugged her shoulders. "I call it superstition, because that's what it is. There isn't any difference, anyway."

"Of course there's a difference. Religion is religion and superstition is superstition. The words don't mean the same, do they, Elderly Teacher?" he asked the oldest of the teachers of Chinese language.

"They are frequently used in a different sense," the old man answered reluctantly.

"They don't mean the same at all," Lu Min declared. "Otherwise, why does our People's Government guarantee religious liberty and at the same time announce that we want to develop science in order to reduce superstition? Unfortunately, sometimes there's superstition mixed with religion, but they're definitely not the same."

"I say they are," Miss Pu sneered. "Tell me a superstition which you consider cannot be called religion."

"Just offhand, I'd say fear of fox fairies."

There was an audible gasp, and Miss Pu's face turned purple. It was a direct hit. The whole school had buzzed earlier in the week over a story that Miss Pu, returning late at night from the Government office, had been followed by what she had at first supposed was a yellow dog. Here the variations of the story began. Some said she later saw it was a real fox. Some went on to add that when she turned into the school gate, there was no longer either dog or fox, but a young lady hurrying down the alley. Still others said that after all the adverse comments Miss Pu had made about buying extra food to nibble on, her bag had been full of sweet cakes and a hungry dog had followed her, that there was no more to it than that but Miss Pu could not say so without confessing to buying the food. Whatever anyone made of the story, this much was sure: Miss Pu had run into the gatehouse stuttering with fright, and dozens of girls had seen her.

For a full minute there was cold silence. Then Lu Min said: " I beg your pardon. I'm sorry I chose that example. Suppose we take instead another common one — the idea that one should not use water freely because he'll have to drink in hell all the water he wasted."

Ling Ning saw Mr. Yang wink at someone across the room.

Miss Pu answered sourly: " I don't care to discuss it further, but I warn you I'm not the only one who's set on clearing the superstitions out of this school, and that means churchgoing, and praying, and all that you choose to call religion. We're going to have pure science."

Ling Ning had forgotten herself in the excitement of an open quarrel between Lu Min and Miss Pu. Suddenly she heard the principal's " Miss Ling."

She had known she would be frightened. Without taking a moment to collect her wits, she launched forth with the sentence she had rehearsed: " My family has always been well-to-do, but now there are only two of us left, my mother and I. She's a capitalist and I'm a worker." She caught Mr. Yang's glance, but was too ill at ease to respond to the encouraging twinkle in his eye.

Ling Ning had been taught at home as a child, by her mother and by tutors, until she was ready for senior high school. She lacked the experience other children had, from their earliest days in primary school, in both speechmaking and dramatics. She was not naturally a good talker. She spoke hesitatingly, conscious always of Miss Pu, but never daring to look at her. As she told about her childhood and education, she directed her remarks to the principal, always courteous and sympathetic. Whenever her glance left him and went around the room, the faces into which she looked showed a sympathetic embarrassment. The speech, which in preparation had seemed to meet Lu Min's counsel, " Drag it out as long as possible," shrank in the telling and was over in a few minutes.

There followed the period in which others might criticize her. She did not know that her inexperience and inadequacy softened the judgments of the older men, whereas any hint of conceit on her part would have made them less kind. One mentioned the music she had played so often on the assembly-room piano with Mr. Yang, and suggested that hereafter they confine themselves to the "new" Chinese music. She wished she could justify herself, but before she could try Mr. Yang spoke up. "We play the music we have. We have no piano arrangements of the 'new' songs."

Mr. Chang, Miss Pu's favorite satellite, spoke: "She breaks up our group solidarity by giving aid where it was not voted. That's entirely contrary to everything we are striving for."

So Miss Pu had learned about the help to the Wang girls! This time Ling Ning answered. "I lent four *wan* to two sisters. As soon as they had gone, I wondered if I ought not to have asked for advice. I doubt if you will have to criticize me for that fault again."

Ling Ning's face burned and her knees trembled as she waited to hear what others might say. The older mathematics teacher said he could name a good point: she worked hard. Someone else added that the girls in the class he sponsored reported that Miss Ling explained her lessons clearly.

The principal spoke, laughing: "In the reports that came in from the students this morning one, from a first-year group, said Miss Ling was so pretty that looking at her helped them study. I'm afraid we can hardly accept that as official Marxism."

"Which group was that?" Miss Pu interrupted, harshly.

"The one whose sponsor was absent this morning—section B. He'll probably straighten them out by next month as to what they're supposed to say." Then he smiled at Ling Ning. "In spite of your statement that your mother is a capitalist and you are a worker, you still have something of the capitalist about you." He wiggled his fingers around his head to indicate her curls, and brushed some imaginary dust meticulously from one shoulder. His mimicry was well done. "You may not think of them as faults, but you should struggle to correct them until you really attain the workers' ways and point of view. When you are serving the people, you forget how you look in your concern for them."

Miss Pu snorted. "There's not a bit of the worker about her. She's all capitalist. Every thought she has belongs to the age of bureaucratic feudalism. She admires her father and grandfather, both old-time officials, and she admires Confucius, whom they followed. She has no progressiveness. It's veneer!" She threw her pencil down on her desk and shut her mouth into a grim line.

"I should like to know," Ling Ning spoke up, and was surprised at the firmness of her voice, "how Miss Pu knows what my thoughts are. She and I have never talked together for more than two minutes, and never about any subject that would give her an inkling of what I think about anything. I think she might well recall Chairman Mao's advice, 'Until you have investigated a subject, do not speak about it.'"

There was an absolute silence. Ling Ning could not guess how her colleagues would look upon her insubordination, but Miss Pu's criticism had seemed to her so unfair that she could not keep silent, no matter what the result might be.

The oldest mathematics teacher asked irrelevantly, "Are you a Christian, Miss Ling?"

"No. My father's family, as Miss Pu says, have always been faithful disciples of Confucius. In my mother's family, some members are Christians, although she herself is not. But she sent me to a Christian senior high school. Being a day pupil, I missed most of the Christian activities. You all know how much freedom of thought there has always been at Yenching. I knew some Christians there and occasionally went to one of their meetings. I know Christian teachings only vaguely, but I respect them. Actually, I've never joined any group — neither the Kuomintang youth organization nor any other, either political or religious. Oh, yes! I belong to the Association for the Advancement of Sino-Soviet Friendship."

The old mathematics teacher nodded his head. "I think we can wait. We'll be able to see whether Miss Ling is progressive or reactionary."

The principal chose to accept this as the final word, and called on Mr. Chen. Ling Ning's trial was over for the present.

It was good to be through her part of the criticism meeting. The talk continued on and on, never hurried except by the principal's patient, "Who will speak?" when the pauses were tiresomely long. Ling Ning herself had nothing to say in criticism of the others. Any time the principal looked inquiringly at her, she shook her head as a child might have done, and he never called on her. By five o'clock all but one of those seated on her side of the room had finished, and the evening session was called for seven. By ten thirty there were still six people left to be criticized, and the principal told them all to come back the next morning at eight.

Two hours were sufficient in the morning to finish, and with a sigh of relief the faculty scattered for a free half day. As they left the room, Mr. Yang was beside Ling Ning. "Let's go for a bicycle ride."

"Not more than an hour! I have hundreds of papers and notebooks to do. But it would be good to get some fresh air."

It was a perfect autumn day. They rode along the auto road that ran from Wangshan toward the east. The land was comparatively flat and the fields beautiful with a plentiful harvest almost ready to be gathered. The road had many travelers who called to their animals or to each other, though there were times when it was quiet enough to hear the sparrows chirping in the willows beside the road. Ling Ning and Mr. Yang pointed out to each other anything that attracted their interest, but after listening to so many hours of talk, the comparatively silent, friendly atmosphere was refreshing.

Four or five miles from the city they came to a beautiful pine grove set back from the road. "Let's rest awhile and then go back," Ling Ning said.

Entering the enclosure, they found a well-cared-for family burying ground. They sat down on the warm stone benches.

"Well, we're through with that for another month!"

Mr. Yang exclaimed. " You did all right, and I can't imagine why Pu is so prejudiced against you. I can't quite make her out. She's got a bad inferiority complex that shows up in the way she bullies people. But how can she, with her background of wealth and position? At least half the teachers in this school are from comfortable families, but no one else is from a rich one like hers. Why does she feel inferior? And besides, why should she pick on you? Maybe you look like somebody she doesn't like."

It was on the tip of Ling Ning's tongue to tell him of the question she had asked, but she said instead, " It's her business to try to make us all progressive."

" She talks about a veneer! What is it the Christians say? ' With what measure you judge, you shall be judged.' Her own veneer's so thin it cracks."

" I'm surprised to hear you say so. She seems to me almost overdiligent."

" Yes! ' Be progressive! ' ' Serve the people! ' If you want to see what a fraud she is, compare her with Lu Min. There's somebody who's real. Of course he's awfully smart, so he gets his own work done and still has time left to help other folks. But that's not all it takes. You've got to care about the other fellow. Lu Min has the imagination to see how your difficulty looks to you, and doesn't minimize it and make you feel small. Without any fuss he helps you in a way that makes it possible for you the next time to handle it yourself. And he doesn't expect even a ' Thank you '! Say whether I'm right."

" Certainly that's the way he's been with me, but — "

" But what? "

" I had a feeling that — well, that he liked me better than some." She knew she was blushing.

" There's something to that," Mr. Yang said, laughing.

“ But you’ll find they all think Lu Min is nice to them because he likes them specially. He does like everybody specially. He won’t say anything unkind about anybody, not even Pu. He doesn’t ‘ serve the masses ’ as a coldhearted duty. He does it the way the Christians preach it, and if all Christians were like him, I’d be one myself. But you take Pu, if she so much as poured you a cup of tea, she’d expect to be praised for serving the people, and want it reported over at Government headquarters.”

“ I was a little worried to see her and Lu Min disagreeing,” Ling Ming said. “ I’m still worried.”

“ There’s going to be a fight all right,” Mr. Yang nodded. “ She means what she says about religion, and Lu Min won’t back down, not with our People’s Government insisting in public statements that the country has religious liberty. They’ll fight and she’ll win. She can have any of us fired and she knows it. So do we. And most of us want to keep our jobs.”

“ When she said ‘ veneer,’ she wasn’t talking about serving the people. She meant that my thinking is reactionary with a veneer of progressiveness. There’s this much truth to it: I’m not a reactionary, but I’m not so progressive as she is. There are other parties in the coalition government. The rest of us feel just as patriotic as the Communists. I think one can be loyal to the People’s Republic of China without being a Communist. She thinks anyone who isn’t a Communist is reactionary.”

“ Then what about her? She’s no Communist! ”

“ She must be.”

“ You mean you think she belongs to the Party? She couldn’t get in if she tried. She’s too ambitious for herself. Do you think if she belonged to the Party Comrade Tung over at the education bureau would pat her on the back and pour tea for her? She'd be expected to do all the spying and tattling she does just as part of her duty. She wouldn't like that. There's too much discipline in the Party for her."

"I don't know her very well. I'm not able to judge whether or not you're right."

"Of course I'm right." Suddenly Mr. Yang burst into loud laughter. "Say! I've just thought of something! Some evening at our study group I'll ask her if she's applied to join the Party. She'll say she's not worthy. When she backs off like that, I'll promise we'll all speak for her. I'll make her apply or lose face. If she gets in, they'll give her some training she needs, and if she doesn't maybe she'll shut up about other people's veneer. I'll really do it."

When Ling Ning reached her bedroom in the Side Court to wash her hands before lunch, she heard low voices in the room next to hers and almost immediately a gentle knock. Her callers were the Wang sisters, who came in stealthily and hurriedly shut the door. Their faces were excited.

"Have you heard what happened at church?" Tientsin asked. "We were just telling Granny Mi."

"No, I just got back from a bicycle ride in the country."

"Miss Pu and Mr. Chang came and spied on the Christians. They stood one on each side of the entrance and wrote everybody's name into little notebooks — I mean everybody from our school."

Ling Ning scarcely knew how to answer. It would never do to discuss other teachers with two students, but she was full of curiosity. Fortunately, the girls needed no questioning.

"I'm in the choir," Tientsin went on, "and we'd been practicing in that building back of the church, and when we came around the corner, there they were. Some of us went on in, but a lot ran back and hid till they had gone. It ruined the anthem, losing all the altos that way, and we had a beautiful one all ready."

"The two teachers didn't go into the church," Little Sister volunteered. "The minister said afterward that he can't stop their coming and standing by the door, or even coming in, so long as they don't try to break up the meeting. He says it's very clever of them, because they can scare the girls away without disobeying the Government. I'm not in the choir. I was already sitting inside, but they saw all of us too, and wrote down our names."

"Were any other teachers there?"

"Just Mr. Lu. I thought the faculty was having its criticism meeting, but they must have been through, because Mr. Lu was at church, same as usual. The principal and the other Christian teachers haven't been coming since summer."

"I think you'd better run along," Ling Ning urged. "It must be time for your lunch."

Such surveillance of the Christian students was unprecedented, Ling Ning suspected. But at the teachers' table it was not mentioned, and Ling Ning kept the news to herself.

She reported the criticism meeting in detail the next time she called on Nurse Sun. They agreed in their concern over the argument between Miss Pu and Lu Min about religion. Like Mr. Yang, Nurse Sun thought there was trouble ahead for Lu Min. She saw no way to help him, but it took her less than a minute to solve the problem of Ling Ning's hair.

"Put it into pigtails," she said. "Lots of the girls wear theirs that way. It wouldn't be unbecoming to you, and it would prove you were trying to be amenable."

The next morning, at the teachers' study hour, Mr. Yang

pulled one of Ling Ning's short braids. Principal Wang's eyes twinkled when he saw her, but he said nothing. To the students' loud and voluble comments, Ling Ning paid no attention. Before the day was half over, her hair was no longer news.

Their vacant period together was the first chance Ling Ning had had to compare impressions with Lu Min since the criticism meeting.

" Have you a little time to talk this morning? " he asked. She nodded and he went on: " You did well on Saturday. The men have been reviewing the affair ever since. No one understands why Miss Pu's criticism of you was so harsh. They all say she has no basis for her conclusions in the way you have acted. You've worked hard at your job and been faithful at study. All you have to do is keep still and continue as you've done. You'll be all right. I wish I could say as much for myself. Wasn't that a terrible social blunder I made about the fox fairies? The idea must have been close to the surface of my subconscious mind, so that when she said ' superstition,' out popped fox fairies. I was horrified and chagrined, but the situation was already past remedy. I wish I could believe it was the last I'll ever hear of it." He shook his head ruefully.

Remembering Mr. Yang's comments, she said, " You two certainly don't agree on religion."

" That's what I want to talk to you about, to see whether we, the two science teachers, have at all similar ideas. Do you think of religion and superstition as identical, as Miss Pu does? "

" My ideas are very vague, because I've never given the matter much thought. But ' offhand,' as you were with the fox fairies," she giggled, " I'd say that I come nearer to agreement with you than with Miss Pu."

" Unlike you, I have spent a lot of both study and reflection on religion. I wonder if you'd let me tell you what I think, to see how nearly parallel our thoughts run."

At her nod, he settled back in his chair and began: " Suppose we start with Miss Pu. She's fighting for science against religion. Marx and Darwin and other great original thinkers of a hundred years ago saw an insoluble conflict there. In their day, religion was likely to be unsympathetic and unyielding to their new scientific discoveries, so much so that they did really have to choose between science and religion as they saw it around them. But a large portion of the Christian Church no longer feels any conflict. Certainly at Yenching we Christian students delighted in science as being a statement of the laws of God's universe. Do your students ask you nearly every day whether the world was created by God or by work? "

" Yes, and I tell them the Marxist theory is that it was created by work, and that's the answer they're to give if I ever ask them the question in an exam — which you may rest assured I won't — and that shuts them up."

After a minute, Lu Min said solemnly: " It's like this. A great Spirit has been working through millenniums in mighty creative deeds of which the end is not yet in sight. Our universe is his creation, and every time we discover a little more about the natural laws under which it functions, we add a little to our scientific knowledge. The creative Spirit is beneficent or he would not have made his work beautiful. He would have made it with hideous clashing colors, or maybe with no colors at all — just black ghastliness. In religion we call the creative Spirit God, and his beneficence, love. We say his love is greater than man's hate. Isn't that as reasonable as to think that work-in-the-abstract created the world? Or if we grant that abstract work created the world, doesn't Work thereby become the very Spirit I've been calling God? Isn't a large part of the conflict caused by differences in interpretation of the words used? "

" Miss Pu's creator is impersonal," Ling Ning suggested.

" Is it essential to its creative power that it should be impersonal? I don't believe it. But for fear you might think I'm making something up, I brought a text along." He took from his desk drawer two identical books, with paper covers carefully pasted over their bindings. As soon as she opened hers, Ling Ning recognized it as a Bible, and understood the caution about the covers. This was a Christian school, but it would be an excuse for criticism of Lu Min if a passing member of the Youth League should see him with a Bible in the teachers' room.

" I'll tell you the pages I want you to read, so it'll be easier for you to find them than if we used the usual method. Let's read the first page in the Book. It is a beautiful poem, not a scientific report. No man was there to take notes. It tells how work created the world."

Quietly he read aloud while her eyes followed the words. When he finished, he asked, " Does that conflict with what you know from science of how this world was evolved through the ages? "

" No, and it's very impressive."

He told her the number of another page, and its chapter and verse — John 5:17. Again he read aloud: " ' My Father worketh hitherto, and I work.' Those are Jesus' words. When he says, ' My Father,' he means the beneficent creative Spirit I've been talking about, and he doesn't minimize the function of work. Jesus had with his ' Father ' a close personal relationship which included a consciousness of being in harmony with his Father's laws. That gave him courage to live. And in so far as we can attain a like relationship we can have a like courage. But these high school girls of ours, with all the difficulties of their adolescent adjustments, are not permitted the assurance that comes from knowing their Heavenly Father. What's going to give them the help they need? Marxism and Mao Tse-tung haven't it to give. I have nothing but pity for them when they reject God as being a 'harmful opiate' or 'ignorant superstition.' Does what I've been talking about sound like superstition to you?"

"No, it's a long way from stories of fox fairies," Ling Ning assured him, "and I find it stimulating. I wonder – Would you give me some more explanations like this? And tell me something more in here I could read?" She held up her Bible.

"You can begin with Mark or Luke, if you've never read them." He flipped over the pages and told her the numbers. "I've been planning to pick out some passages that correlate with our daily study of Communism. That might be profitable for you too. We can compare Christian and Marxist teachings. Marx had the advantage of eighteen hundred years of history."

Later in the day, Ling Ning found her thoughts returning again and again to Lu Min's statement of his faith, and the more she thought about what he had said, the more reasonable it seemed to her.

The next day, true to his promise, Lu Min was ready to start the study. He had paper on which he had jotted down similarities between Communism and Christianity – similarities such as make some people say that Communism is really a religion. He read them off to her:

"A hero, whose words have become a holy book, who is an infallible authority, and who must be venerated if not actually worshiped; a close association of all believers, separate from the rest of the world; a utopia of the abundant life which is to be the reward of the faithful; a call to complete surrender of the whole life to the cause, giving up home and family, and practicing self-denial; a call to absolute faith, acceptance of the whole teaching with no criticism or variation; a conversion that makes of the believer a new creature, sometimes even giving up his old name and taking a new one; confession of faults and constant attempt at self-improvement; raising the position of women and outcasts; preaching of the deceitfulness of riches, and against being greedy for things; service to the common people — each a total philosophy, a way of living, which demands exclusive loyalty."

He also had a list of page numbers — short passages which they read together quietly. They discussed how similar or how different they were from the Communist teaching they had learned that morning in faculty study hour.

Day after day Ling Ning gave a few minutes to this project of Lu Min's and felt that her growing interest in religion was more mature than her earlier indifference. They took some pains not to be observed as doing anything different from what they had always done at the morning hour. They were especially careful not to let anyone notice their Bibles, and when they left, carried them away with them, knowing that students came at will and ransacked the teachers' desks. Every evening Ling Ning read a little in the Bible Lu Min had given her. After she had read it, she always stuck it into the top of the box under her bed. She did not analyze her motives. What she read was not all new, but she was finding it interesting to put her scattered knowledge of Christianity into the new framework that Lu Min was making for her. His analyses were always stimulating;

the more so as she learned more about the Christian religion and so had a better foundation for further understanding. Even the faculty study hours on Communism were changed and enlivened for her by this fresh approach. She had very little time for it, but spent no more than she had formerly used in playing the piano with Mr. Yang. These minutes added flavor and zest to the rest of the day.

Chapter 4

October first is the anniversary of the establishment of the People's Republic of China. Before the middle of September, plans were well developed for a three-day celebration in Wangshan. At the Girls' School, the burden fell largely on Mr. Chen, the physical director, because the main feature was a two-day track meet, in which the classes of all the schools in the county would compete.

Besides regular track events, there would be, in a different part of the grounds, another competition in which each class would perform some athletic demonstration, striving for that which was most original and most effective. The class sponsors naturally had a large share in suggesting the demonstrations and in training the performers.

The simple *yang ko,* or rustic dance, that had come in with the Liberation had already lost its interest. The girls wanted something more elaborate, their wishes going far beyond their abilities. Ling Ning, having at other meetings seen their incompetence when doing things in unison, happily remembered a stunt of her Yenching days. It was actually only the *yang ko,* which they all knew how to do, elaborated by a performance with some very large red paper hats. It proved to be easily within the powers of her little first-year girls, and its gaudiness, and their satisfaction in doing it so well at their practices, pleased them beyond anything Ling Ning could have hoped.

The meet would take place on the Boys' School grounds, which were the largest and best equipped of any in Wangshan. All the teachers were called upon to be assistants to the physical director. So were a large number of the older students, especially the officers of the Student Union and of the Youth League. They had taken part in so many track meets that they needed no coaching.

On one of the rare occasions when Ling Ning found Mr. Chen at his desk next to hers, she asked him what he wanted her to do.

" Anything you like, Miss Ling, just so you help. We'll need everybody. Such a mob of children! "

" I can read and write. Have you any job of checking the names of the contestants? "

He looked at his lists. " Yes, that'll be a good one for you. I'll put you down for the broad jump. There aren't many names to check — it takes each group so long — but the place is near the goal of the races, so you can see them and not miss all the excitement of your first meet at Wangshan."

Ling Ning thanked him, conscious of how thoughtful her colleagues were. She found that Lu Min and Mr. Yang were assigned to judging the races. They considered it a very difficult post because they would be so constantly busy, and there was often a chance for a difference of opinion. But they had both done it before and were well satisfied, because it was sure to be interesting.

As the day approached, lessons became a secondary matter. Ling Ning, upon asking her third-year girls to write in chemistry class a short assignment she had told them to memorize, was yelled at. " We don't write any more quizzes until after the track meet! " At study hour she remarked to

Mr. Chen, " The students take the practice for their track meet quite seriously, don't they? "

He looked at her sharply. " I wondered if you were joking. The only reason they get any points at all is because their rivals don't practice either. The boys are all right, but the girls have very low standards."

She told him about her chemistry class.

" That's because this week I've been taking them over to the boys' grounds to get used to the track. They imagine they're working overtime. We do have one good little runner, a new first-year girl from Tientsin. Her name's Wang, and the girls all call her ' Little Sister.' She's a natural runner."

" She's in my class! " Ling Ning exclaimed, pleased. " I'll be on the lookout for her. Maybe we'll get some points. My girls say they don't stand a chance against the older ones."

" They do have just this chance: they don't take anything for granted and they try harder to the very end. Oh, now I remember! Little Sister is one of the Wang girls you were criticized for helping. I hope the school will give her free tuition next term. I'd like a chance to give her some training. Maybe I can talk Miss Pu into it if I start early."

" It's worth something to the school to have good athletes."

" Naturally," Mr. Chen smiled, " that would be my opinion. I don't think we're so good! We've taken over the Soviet ways of doing things, including their Swedish drills. I don't know how the Russian students do them, but if the Swedes could see our girls it would make an international incident — all those flopping arms and legs, with no precision of movement anywhere! The girls themselves think they're wonderful. They'd want to mob me if I should say to them what I'm saying now to you."

" Our students have the same fault in their science study. They don't want to be held to close discipline. They like to think that anything that they say goes."

" Or that by repeating it, they can make it so. Well, you're young. Maybe you'll be able to keep in their good graces by seeing things as a teen-ager does. But I'm twenty-eight, and that's too old. Besides, I've been as far as Shanghai. That's a handicap too. I can't help knowing there are other ways of doing things besides the way we do them in Wangshan, and that it's conceivable that some of the other ways are better. Along with all our talk of criticism and self-criticism, we're in danger of letting it be just talk and of being actually so conceited we won't grant that any other country can do things as well as we. Now there's a reactionary speech for you! It isn't that I think China won't come out all right in the end. Of course we will. Or that I question the leadership of Chairman Mao and the rest. They're fine. But it makes me mad, having to agree to everything every fourteen-year-old in Wangshan says or have my patriotism doubted! "

Despite Mr. Chen's disparagement of their athletic ability, the occasion was one of wild excitement for the Wangshan students. This excitement aroused the populace, so that on the first day of the meet a big crowd filled the bleachers.

The meet was managed with considerable ceremony. The participants entered the field school by school. Flag-bearers led, carrying as many huge red flags as the school owned — four or six, or even eight or ten. Behind them danced the gaily bedizened waist-drum corps, beating an elaborate rhythm on their waist drums, newly fashionable since the Liberation. Finally came the contestants, marching by fours. The gaudy red and yellow of the flags, with the blue of the school uniforms, made the whole field bright and gay.

When all were in place, there followed the salute to the flag and the singing of the national anthem. A speech by the head of the education bureau launched the program. From then on, a loud-speaker was constantly calling the contestants or announcing the winners. This, with the aid of mimeographed programs, kept comparative order in what at times appeared to be complete confusion.

Ling Ning's task was an easy one, and as Mr. Chen had promised, she had time and opportunity to see the finish of a good many of the races. From where she was she could not see the class stunts; but when her own class was called, she left to direct them, and was gratified that they had never before done so well.

It was at the close of the second day that the track meet ran into trouble. A dozen or more of the minor officials who, like Ling Ning, had finished their own duties, were crowded around the finish of the races where the final relay was attracting everyone's attention. To the delighted amazement of Ling Ning's class of first-year girls, and the loudly expressed vexation of almost all the older girls, her section C was close to winning the meet.

Little Sister had entered all the shorter races, and won first in every one she had run. A long-legged, spindly tomboy, known as Pigtails, had also made a good score. However the high total was not the work of these two girls alone, but was the result of someone's having placed in nearly every event. Mr. Chen had said their chance stood in their trying hard. They had tried very hard. With so much at stake on this last race, excitement was high as runners representing six classes were placed at their posts for the final test.

They were all Ling Ning's students. But the little girls were especially hers, since she was their sponsor. Ling Ning's eyes never left her own runners as at first they fell slightly behind and gave Little Sister a handicap on the last stretch. But how she ran! She passed one and then another of the competitors.

It was over so soon! And although an older athlete and Little Sister finished practically together, Ling Ning was sure Little Sister was a few inches ahead.

The little girls screamed shrilly with joy. But so also did one section of the third-year girls — the one whose runner, as Ling Ning had seen it, came in second. Ling Ning knew the girl as a very popular member of the Youth League.

It was only a matter of a few minutes before it was evident that there was a question about the winner. Ling Ning, standing at one side, watched the judges surrounded by shouting, gesticulating students. In the middle of the uproar, she could see Lu Min, Mr. Yang, and Miss Pu's friend Chang. The argument was taken up by all the students until the clamor was deafening. It was not for Ling Ning to decide. Small as her part had been in the track meet, she was tired. She started back to her room.

Some of the little girls, seeing her, came crowding around her. " Who do you think won? " they asked breathlessly.

" I thought Little Sister won," she answered, " but there seems to be some doubt about it. We'll soon hear how the judges decide."

" Maybe the judges can't decide. You know the one we call the Empress, chairman of the Student Union? She says she doesn't care what those judges say, the victory goes to the third-year class. She says Little Sister didn't get in first. She says they all saw it, plainer than the judges."

Another piped up: " Mr. Lu says Little Sister was first, but that man from the country says she was second, and now Mr. Yang won't say either way. You saw her win, didn't you, Miss Ling? "

This time Ling Ning did not commit herself, but too many of them had heard her first statement, and passed the word along. " Miss Ling says Little Sister won! "

Ling Ning kept trying to quiet them, to persuade them to wait until the official decision was known, but they told everyone they met: " Our class won. Little Sister was first. Miss Ling says so."

She finally got away into the seclusion of the Side Court. Later, at the teachers' supper table, everyone avoided mentioning the meet, but once outside Ling Ning murmured to Lu Min, " What did you decide about that relay? "

" It isn't decided. There's an awful row."

Others began to talk about it and Ling Ning escaped. Since for once there was no evening " study," she enjoyed the quiet of her little room, hearing only distantly the shouting and confusion in the Big Court.

The next day was also a holiday, a real one, with neither big meetings nor small discussion groups. Granny Mi reported that the whole school was still quarreling over the track meet. Ling Ning washed her clothes and her hair, caught up on several piles of notebooks, and went shopping. She disliked arguments and intended to avoid this one.

In the afternoon, before she went for her customary call on Nurse Sun, she got again from Granny Mi the latest news about the meet. Empress was not only chairman of the Student Union, but also one of the leading members of the Youth League. So were the third-year runner and most of the older girls she represented. Mr. Chang, though not a judge of the races, had taken an active part in the quarrel, even going so far as to say that Lu Min's decision in favor of Little Sister was really motivated by dislike for the League. As if anyone would dare to oppose the Youth

League! The decision was finally given to the third-year class. The younger girls continued to seethe with ill will because of what they considered an injustice, and the others because of what they chose to interpret as a threat to Youth League prestige.

The next morning, to Ling Ning's surprise, Lu Min showed no bitterness over the decision. He tacitly agreed that he thought the meet had been wrongly judged and that he himself had been unjustly accused, but he refused to be angry about it.

"I don't see how you can take it so calmly," Ling Ning protested. "I wish I had such self-control!"

"It isn't self-control. It's a point of view, and I can explain it easily." Lu Min took his Bible, opened it in the middle, and after searching a minute or two, told her a page number. "Psalm 37, the seventh verse," he directed, and read quietly: "'Rest in the Lord, and wait patiently for him: fret not thyself because of him who prospereth in his way, because of the man who bringeth wicked devices to pass,' and the fifth verse, 'Commit thy way unto the Lord; trust also in him; and he shall bring it to pass.' That's clear enough!"

"It still takes self-control."

Lu Min was again turning pages, and when he told her the number, she found that the passage was in the thirteenth chapter of Matthew. "The situation Jesus describes is just what we have here, allowing for the metaphors," Lu Min said. "I read this occasionally to remind myself to have patience." Again he read quietly, while Ling Ning followed the words in her own book.

"'The kingdom of heaven is likened unto a man that sowed good seed in his field: but while men slept, his enemy came and sowed tares also among the wheat, and went away.

But when the blade sprang up, and brought forth fruit, then appeared the tares also. And the servants of the householder came and said unto him, Sir, didst thou not sow good seed in thy field? whence then hath it tares? Wilt thou then that we gather them up? But he saith, Nay; lest haply while ye gather up the tares, ye root up also the wheat with them. Let both grow together until the harvest: and in the time of harvest I will say to the reapers, Gather ye together first the tares, and bind them in bundles to burn them: but gather the wheat into my barn.' "

He looked at her and smiled. " Isn't the world an interesting experiment? If we're scientists at all, we ought to try to watch it out — as long as we're here to watch — as God is watching it, with faith that in the end it'll come out right. When I run into injustice that I can't control, I come back to these verses and try to prove that I'm worthy of being a scientist by showing patience."

In June, Korea caught the attention of the world, and was never thereafter absent from the news in China, whether by radio or newspaper. There was from the first strong opposition to the action of the United Nations in sending soldiers, and this action was blamed entirely on the United States. No Wangshan students ever said that the Northern Koreans were fighting against the United Nations. They always said it was against " invading Americans," or " American aggression." In fact, this was true all over China, to the extent that an American teacher in Nanking was actually deported for arguing with her students that the opponent of the Northern Koreans was the United Nations and not the United States as they insisted.

Feeling ran very high from the first. By autumn the phrase, " *K'ang mei! Yuan ch'ao!* " — " Resist America!

Aid Korea! " — had become a national slogan.

Through the summer and early fall there had been swift visits at the Wangshan Girls' School by former students who had joined the Army and gone south many months before at the time of the Liberation. Whenever such a one appeared in the school courtyard, she was instantly surrounded by her former schoolmates, who listened eagerly to her tales of adventure in faraway provinces of China. The girl soldiers told of long days of marching which took them almost the whole length of the land; and if occasionally the name of some Wangshan boy or girl who had died or been killed in battle was mentioned, there would be a silence, and then hate for the Kuomintang would flare up all the fiercer.

Now the soldiers were all returning from the south, gaily, apparently never regretting the education they had given up to join the Communist Army. They received much adulation from their former schoolmates, and took it as though they were used to it. And why not? Were they not the heroes of New China? They could stop only briefly. They were marching north with their companies. Nothing was said as to where the Liberation Army was going or why.

The newspaper told of the retreat of the Northern Koreans, and then, day by day, enraged the students with reports of bombings by American planes on the Chinese side of the Amur. The stories gave complete details: the hour, the minute, the type of plane, the number of bombs dropped, the damage done, a description of the persons injured or killed, and interviews with their neighbors. Daily the students waited after lunch to hear the reading of that day's news in the newspaper that had just come from Peking. Since only one at a time could look at the paper and no one was willing to wait, whoever had it read aloud.

To "Resist America! Aid Korea!" were added with even more feeling: "*Pao chia! Wei kuo!*" – "Guard our homes! Protect our country!" Patriotism became an all-absorbing emotion, and anything that was not clearly directed toward the protection of the northeastern frontier seemed of no importance. When the Liberation Army reached the border, the news of Chinese "volunteers" rushing into Korea to help the Northerners was received with acclaim, and their later victories with rejoicing and pride. China need not fear the paper tiger of the United States while such heroes were ready to protect their fatherland!

It was not long before the Wangshan students were being mobilized to carry to their less literate neighbors the news they themselves read so avidly. The educational department announced that they were to go to all the nearby villages. Teachers and pupils alike welcomed the opportunity to express in action the emotion that was constantly stirred and had been bottled up so long.

Ling Ning and Lu Min were carried along in the rush of preparations. Each had a class to sponsor, and they were called on for help of every kind. With no less friendliness when they were together, they saw far less of each other.

Plays had to be written and rehearsed to give the news in a lively form that would appeal to the old villagers. Dialogues and dances must be invented and practiced. As for patriotic songs, everybody had to know all of them, that having been the policy of the Government right along – to print a new propaganda song in the newspaper and then play it constantly on the radio, and have it taught in every school and study class until everybody from five to fifty had added it to his repertoire.

As the day for the first excursion approached – they had no holidays on which to carry on their patriotic work –

often more than half the girls would be absent from class, sending oral messages that they were " busy."

Finally the making of posters was added to the other activities. Only a few students had enough artistic ability to draw pictures, but everybody could write with a large Chinese brush pen. On hundreds of strips of brightly colored paper each class wrote slogans to be pasted on the walls everywhere they went. The slogans included the now well-known: " Resist America! Help Korea! Guard our homes! Protect our country! " There were many others: " Ten thousand years to Chairman Mao! Ten thousand years to the Chinese Communist Party! Ten thousand years to Sino-Soviet friendship! Ten thousand years to the Liberation Army! Down with American imperialism! Down with American capitalism! Down with lovers of America! Don't fear the American paper tiger! Oppose rearming Japan. Unite! In union is strength! "

Collections were taken to buy flour for paste, and washbasins were spoken for in which to make and carry the paste.

The day came, clear and sunny as October days in North China are likely to be. Breakfast was eaten in excited gaiety. The waist-drum corps, dressed in their all-white costumes, with red bands over their shoulders to hold up the drums, and red and yellow silk handkerchiefs tied to the ends of their drumsticks, performed elaborate *yang ko* while they beat:

Tum te-te-te-te tum tum.
Tum te-te-te-te tum.
Tum te-te-te-te tum tum.
Tum te-te-te-te tum.

Away they went, through the suburb and out into the country. The country was at its loveliest with fall colors, the yellow leaves not yet having fallen and the russet crops not yet all gathered. The marchers took a short cut across a dry river bed and scrambled up the opposite steep bank. Soon Lu Min and several other men teachers were stretching out a hand to help the girls clamber up, amid much shrieking and laughing. Anxiety over what might be happening in Korea was forgotten in the fun of a holiday in the country in the beautiful autumn sunshine.

Soon their ways parted, each group going to the village to which it had been assigned, where it would carry out dutifully the program it had prepared and return wearily in the late afternoon.

After a few days of lessons, during which they again took time to write innumerable slogans, they would go on another such expedition, to another set of villages. Thus by using all the students in both high schools, the local Government soon reached with its propaganda to all the villages within walking distance. Soon even the old farmers were saying fluently: "Resist America! Aid Korea! Guard our homes! Protect our country!"

Chapter 5

The propaganda excursions to the country ran into November. The days became shorter and often it was nearly dark, and uncomfortably cold, by the time the students and their teachers arrived back at school. On such occasions there was no study hour in the evening; they could all go to bed early and be ready for classes the next day. To these the pupils came entirely unprepared and often restive at the thought of lessons. It never occurred to Ling Ning to do other than teach as much as she could. Her classes were far behind the schedule she had turned in to the education department of the Government when school opened. Teaching, though now not such a new experience, was much more difficult than it had been at first. No matter how tired she was, she tried to think up something that would catch the waning interest.

Unwillingly she came to the conclusion that it was not in her imagination only that some of the older girls were increasingly discourteous. There was no doubt about it on the morning when, in the middle of something she was saying, the girl known as Empress stood up and without asking to speak, said: "This is no way to teach chemistry! You ought to have taught us first off all those letters that stand for things. We ought to have memorized the whole list in the back of the book, and then maybe we'd know what you're talking about."

Ling Ning was so taken aback that she answered nothing but stood before the class, looking at the girl and trying to think what she ought to do. Finally, not having been able to think of anything, almost mechanically she went on with what she had been saying, treating the interruption as though it had never happened. Slight giggles rippled over the class. These also she ignored and went on with the lesson.

Afterward, looking for Lu Min in the teachers' room, she found instead Mr. Yang, and described the incident to him.

"I wouldn't think you'd have any trouble understanding that," he said. "It's perfectly plain to me. You're chosen for some petty persecution by the Youth League. I think if you ask Lu Min you'll find they've been doing that sort of thing in his classes ever since the track meet."

"What ought I to have done?"

"Just what you did. They're trying to make you angry enough to say something you ought not to say. If you get angry and sputter, they've succeeded. If you look angry, they have hopes. But if you act as though you never saw or heard it, they're frustrated."

"I suppose that's so. But I wonder what started them."

"That's easy too. Pu told them you're reactionary. But don't ask me how to win their hearts. That I can't tell you. Once they put a hat on you, it's hard to do anything about it."

"But it's so unjust!" Ling Ning protested. "I'm not reactionary! I work just as hard as anybody else in this school at everything the Government asks us to do. I'm just as hothearted in resisting America and helping Korea as the noisiest of them. Just because I don't stand in the middle of the courtyard and scream — "

Mr. Yang grinned at her. " I'm not the one who put the hat on you. It was Pu. And she's done it, not because you are really reactionary, but because she doesn't like you and she's got the upper hand. With all her little apprentices in the Youth League doing whatever she tells them to do, I don't think you can do anything about it. It's hard luck, but it could happen to any of us."

Lu Min, when she told him about it, confessed that similar incidents happened often in his classes, being sometimes criticism, but more often taking the form of difficult questions on controversial subjects which he had no time to answer even had he known how. He agreed with Mr. Yang that the best reaction was to ignore the discourteous elements. " They don't do it every day," he said, " and each time we manage not to show irritation, it helps toward a victory the next time. I hope they'll eventually get tired of it."

The last excursion was to a village four miles away. Unfortunately, there was a strong north wind, and Ling Ning and her little girls were both chilled and exhausted when at last, after dark, they returned to school. It had not been fun like the earlier trips, but the drudgery was done faithfully and loyally because it was for their country.

As they came in, the gateman gave Ling Ning a letter from her mother. She put it into her pocket with the happy anticipation that as soon as she had eaten and could relax for the evening, she would have her mother's letter to enjoy.

But when she had read it, her eagerness was chilled by the news she found there:

"You will be shocked, as we all were, to hear of the arrest of your uncle, my oldest brother. As you know, I had not been in the habit of visiting at his home very frequently, but I had gone at once to take him your letter telling of the warning from the abbot at the Temple of the Blue Lake. He said he knew of no way to deter such a man as that Wu. He felt sure that running away was impossible, and that anything he could do or say would only start trouble, so that his best hope was to avoid calling attention to himself. Because I'd been warned about him, I've gone to their house oftener, and I happened to be there when the police came and took him away. He is charged with being a reactionary, and with having enriched himself at the expense of the people of Wangshan.

"On this occasion he had no opportunity to discuss anything with any of us, but earlier, after he read your letter, his thought was of you — that there might be danger for you there on his account. So he sent you his strictest command and most earnest entreaty that you make no inquiry or in any way let it be known that there is any relationship between you. Your doing so could not help him, since even without it he rests assured of your loyal love, and it might put upon you a shadow which could lead you into misfortune.

"Your aunt is prostrated. Your cousins and uncles are trying to find some way to effect his release. This may not be possible. The report is that he is being taken immediately to Wangshan to be tried there, and that his accusers are already waiting his arrival.

"Think of him, an old man used to the comforts of a good home, traveling and imprisoned in this cold weather! That would be enough to endure. But from the bearing and talk of the police who arrested him, his punishment is likely to be severe — could even be death — to be an example to others and frighten them, now that the Government is in the midst of its campaign against reactionaries.

"My heart is heavy with anxiety, not only for him but for you, for fear you have carelessly let fall information about our summer in Wangshan which may implicate you in your uncle's misfortune. So I repeat his injunction as my own — don't imagine there is any way you can help him. Being near at hand does not mean there is anything you can do for him, but only that you are near danger. Do be careful! Destroy this letter at once. Then don't give yourself away by any expression that indicates that we are in trouble. If that seems to you hardhearted or in any way unworthy, remember that it is your uncle's expressed wish and may prove to be the last thing you can do for him. If he thought he was bringing any danger on you, it would add unbearably to his unhappiness.

"You will be interested to know that, oddly enough, during the hour before the police came, though he had no premonition that they were actually at hand, he was talking about his life — how last spring he had finished the full cycle of sixty years, and felt that his life was complete and that he would be well content whenever it ended. He said he regretted only one thing, that, being a Christian, he had always accepted the spiritual comfort of his religion without making any effort to help anyone else share its consolations, not even his dearest and nearest. He said he had in that regard been like a Confucianist, not like a good Christian. It was an odd coincidence that his talk should have been along such lines, and I am glad he shared with us those thoughts of his because he may never have another chance.

"Now, having read, burn this at once. I trust you to do it, and to obey faithfully your uncle's wishes."

There were a few more words. As though unconscious of what she did, Ling Ning put the letter in the middle of the brick floor and lighted it with a match.

She was stunned. She did not cry, but sat looking dully at the opposite wall while through her mind ran pictures of that summer at Wangshan. Again she saw her uncle in his home in Peking, a cultured old-style gentleman for whom life had always brought success and honor. She remembered him through the years, from her earliest childhood. She called up more recent events — those since she had become one of the adults of the family. The memories would all have been happy ones if they had not been overshadowed by the present misfortune, which her mother looked upon with such fear.

Ling Ning slept badly and anticipated the hour when she could tell Lu Min about her uncle's trouble. She was glad she had one friend in Wangshan who knew about him. Though she had known Lu Min so short a time, she did not doubt him. Everything she knew about him proclaimed him trustworthy.

The minute he saw her, he exclaimed anxiously, "What's happened?"

"Do I show it so plainly as that?" Ling Ning asked, alarmed. Her mother had specifically cautioned her on this very point. "I'm glad you told me. I must compose my face."

She bent over her desk, apparently looking intently at a

book. In low tones which only he could hear, she told him all that was in her mother's letter. She felt his sympathy as instant and deep as she had known it would be. Tears came to her eyes, and her voice trembled.

After she had finished they sat in silence, and then his voice came quietly: "I think your mother is quite right. You must not do anything that could connect you with your uncle. But I am free. No one can find any connection between him and me, and there's no reason why anyone should invent one. I can inquire, and I promise you I won't bungle anything I do and get you into danger."

With that they looked at each other, pity in his eyes and gratitude in hers.

"Because I shall have to be so careful, I may not be able to do much — I might not anyway — but I'll tell you every morning whatever I find out, and you won't feel so much, as you do now, that you are neglecting your uncle. He probably came to Wangshan as fast as your mother's letter, but I doubt if anyone is allowed to talk to him, even if one knew in which of the several local police stations he is imprisoned. This noon I'll make an excuse to go into the city and wander around through some of the main streets and see what I see."

"I hadn't thought of your doing anything of that sort," Ling Ning said. "I just knew I mustn't. I haven't gone into the city much, and it would be sure to cause comment. It's good of you."

At chemistry class a girl in the front seat said solicitously: "You look pale, Miss Ling. I think yesterday's excursion must have tired you." Ling Ning almost grasped at this good excuse for whatever outward signs she might be giving of her worry. But intuition warned her.

"Oh, no," she said, "what we've been doing is very, very

little. Think of the volunteers in Korea! "

The girl turned around and looked at Empress. Empress raised her eyebrows. Ling Ning was well satisfied not to have fallen into that trap.

In the late afternoon a half hour with Nurse Sun sent Ling Ning back to her room refreshed. As she came through the small gate into the Side Court she was surprised to see a light in her room and hear the chatter and laughter of schoolgirls. She knew she had locked her door, as she always did. Had Granny Mi, who had the other key, let them in?

The idea was promptly negatived by Granny Mi herself, who shook her palm back and forth to indicate that Ling Ning was to ignore her presence. It was evident she was agitated, and irritated, but did not want to become involved in whatever was afoot.

Ling Ning opened her door and stepped in. The little room was filled by seven or eight girls, sitting in chairs or on the bed or squatting on the floor, each with a drawer from the desk or a little pile of books which she was examining.

" I have callers? " Ling Ning inquired politely.

Not at all flustered by her arrival, several of the girls looked up. Empress spoke. " We're a committee of the Youth League. We're doing volunteer service for our country in looking for reactionary literature and writings."

" You won't find any here," Ling Ning answered.

" Oh, but we have already," one girl said, flourishing a letter. " Here's a friend of yours " — she looked at the signature — " Chang Lo-i who teaches in Tangshan. She complains that the members of the Youth League in her school are nosy and rude, slaves of the politics teacher. Why does she think she can write that way to you? Because you had already written something just as bad or worse to her about us! "

" I had done nothing of the sort! " Ling Ning contradicted her indignantly. " I've never written her a word since I came here! "

The girl smirked and gave a little grunt. Another said: " Of course she'll lie about it. Don't pay any attention to her. Hurry up and read the rest of those letters."

" I hate this Youth League! " Ling Ning thought. " That's one point where I'm reactionary and don't care. Maybe if they were like the descriptions of them in the Government announcements I shouldn't feel this way. On paper they're so loyal and patriotic and have such high ideals! But what these girls do to prove their patriotism I consider officious and egotistic. They think their coming in here this way is the wonderful new liberty, and I think it's unjustifiable interference in my private affairs. I hate this helplessness while children maul my things and read my letters."

Letters! Ling Ning looked at the box under the bed. Under no circumstances must these Youth League girls be allowed to get the little bundle of her mother's letters that were in that box. How fortunate it was that the last one, about her uncle, had been burned! But how utterly foolish she had been to keep them. Unlike the one they had found from Chang Lo-i, her mother's indicated clearly what she had written about the happenings at school. She had often made comments more critical than the phrase they objected to: " Nosy and rude, slaves of the politics teacher." In the box was also the Bible Lu Min had given her – not incriminating, to be sure, but obnoxious to these girls and sure to be put on the record against her. She was glad that the box had a good foreign lock and that lately she had got into the habit of locking it and carrying the key. But what good would the lock do? They would simply demand her key. In a panic she waited for what she knew was coming.

One of the girls, having finished reading all the papers in one of the drawers pushed them together and forced the drawer back into the desk. "We leave everything just the way we found it," she said. Ling Ning was too distracted to wonder how long it would take her to straighten out the mess.

Another girl finished a pile of books she had been going through page by page, reading the marginal notes, and threw them down on the desk. Empress was nearly through reading the letters she was working on. Several others completed their tasks, and still nothing had been said about the box under the bed. Ling Ning wished there were grounds for hope that they had not noticed it, or that one might think that the others had inspected it.

Finally one girl went over and kicked the box. "Where's the key?" she asked bluntly. "None of ours would work."

Ling Ning had always thought her a comparatively mild child, but in the presence of the others, she was violently truculent.

"That has clothes in it," Ling Ning told her. "I'm afraid they're reactionary. I've had some of them since I was in high school, five or six years, so of course they're old style. But I'll be making them over as I have need for them. I'm wearing the only ones I have that are up-to-date."

By this time Empress had finished. "You don't need to talk about them. Just give us the key and we'll soon know more about them."

The moment had come! Ling Ning either had to give them the key or refuse to do so, and whichever she did she was sure to get into trouble. They all looked at her with hostile eyes. She stood by the door trembling, but outwardly calm.

No one moved. Then came a distant sound — the supper bell. Ling Ning heard it and hoped. Slowly her hopes became reality. The hearty appetites of youth ordered departure, and the nearest girl started for the door.

"Oh, well!" she said. "Her old clothes!"

"At least we got this letter," the finder gloated.

With no more ado they were gone!

Ling Ning scarcely breathed until she was sure they were out of the court. Then, hastily locking her door, she opened the chest, took out the Bible that was on top and hid it under some of the papers that had been examined. She thrust her mother's letters into the stove. Locking the box again, she opened the door to let out the smell of burning paper. She poked the letters until they could no longer be recognized as letters, and went to her own supper. She felt sure the girls would not come back, but it was a relief to have nothing she need hide.

It was well she had taken the precaution. When she came out of the teachers' dining room, she found Empress and two other third-year girls waiting for her.

"We are ashamed that we did not do our patriotic work more thoroughly," Empress said. "We'll still look in the box."

Her heart light, Ling Ning dared argue. "I told you it's full of clothes, and it's quite unnecessary for you to look at them."

Her opposition made Empress suspicious. "Will you go with us, or give us the key?"

"It's time for evening study," Ling Ning again demurred.

"We won't keep you long. Or you can give us the key."

" No, I'll go if I must. I'm afraid you'll make fun of my old-fashioned clothes to the other students. There's absolutely nothing else in there."

She heard one whisper to the other: " She's mighty anxious not to let us see what's in the box. We mustn't let her fool us."

Ling Ning walked back as fast as she could. She quickly unlocked her door. After all the suspense she had suffered, it was fun to rouse their hopes that they were going to catch her in some way. She pulled the box out from under the bed.

" Really, you don't need to look."

" ' Nothing but clothes in it,' " Empress mimicked her. " We're going to look in that box, and there's no use in your trying to put us off."

Slowly Ling Ning unlocked it and stepped back. Such a scramble! They snatched out the garments, shook them, felt in the pockets, pinched all the hems and seams, and held them against the light trying to find incriminating evidence. Then, in disgust, they threw the clothes one by one on the bed. There were not after all very many, and in a short time they came to the bottom of the box.

" There was nothing in there at all but some old-fashioned clothes," Empress pronounced angrily, as though Ling Ning had promised her a great deal more.

Ling Ning had no inclination to say, " I told you so." She only hoped they would leave soon, before one of them should notice the faint odor of burned paper she thought she could detect.

" Well, that's what she said all the time," a second girl answered in a matter-of-fact voice. " You're the one who was sure she was lying."

" We really must go back to the study hour, if you're

through," Ling Ning said gently, interrupting what looked like the beginning of an argument.

"Yes, we're through," Empress grumbled, and led the way out.

Ling Ning sighed, but as she sighed she smiled. She was over that hurdle too.

Chapter 6

Lu Min began to report the next morning as soon as he and Ling Ning were seated at their desks with their heads bent over their books.

"When I promised you to find out about your uncle," he said, "I had no plan. After a little I thought maybe I could get our pastor to help me without telling him why. Your uncle may have attended this church, though I've never heard it mentioned, but his being a Christian would elicit the minister's special interest. Then I decided that first I'd go myself into the city to reconnoiter, before I spoke to him about it, so that I could claim some source of information.

"Well, yesterday noon I went the back way into the city to all the likely places, like the barber shop. I read the posted notices, and loitered by them to see what men were talking about. Nowhere did I hear one mention of your uncle. Then absent-mindedly, being disappointed, and trying to think what to do, I came back the front way, and whom do you think I ran into?"

"I couldn't guess!"

"At the front gate of our school, selling persimmons from a wheelbarrow, was the abbot of the Temple of the Blue Lake."

"How odd!"

"That's what I thought. He saw me a long way off, and as soon as I was near, he beckoned to me. He told me he's been there two days waiting for one of us to pass in or out, thinking it was better not to send in a message. He left his food stand outside the temple with another old monk, and came to Wangshan especially on your uncle's account, hoping to do something for him, or at least to comfort him in some way."

"Then it wasn't just talk when he said he was a friend of my uncle's."

"He wants to be sure you know all he's found out – not very much, but lots more than we know. He's going to move his wheelbarrow to where our alley comes out by the hospital. It's a better place for him, and more convenient for you. I promised him you'd go over there before supper and he could talk to you. He's a smart old fellow. The persimmon business is not entirely a blind. He's making his living as he goes."

"We'd better develop a sudden passion for persimmons," Ling Ning suggested.

"I thought of that. The wheelbarrow is a good idea because he's able to move around without attracting attention, and can ask all the questions he likes. He's found out that your uncle is in the police headquarters in the old yamen."

"Where he lived as the official!"

"Eleven villages are accusing him, and as many more individuals, and the big accusation meeting for the public is tomorrow, Saturday."

"Oh!" Ling Ning drew in a deep breath.

"You remember the day we were at the temple, how the abbot said your uncle had an enemy named Wu? He was a minor official who became exceedingly ' progressive ' after the Liberation. But because your uncle once punished him for bribery he has always carried the thought of revenge. When the People's Government started their campaign against reactionaries, he saw his chance. He has mustered everyone he can find who had any reason to be disgruntled with your uncle's treatment. When the police called meetings of the villages and told them to accuse anyone they disliked, most of the villagers hated to accuse their neighbors even in cases of injustice, for fear they would themselves be accused. Then this Wu, or whoever was attending a village meeting as his accomplice, would make a speech about your uncle. They got eleven villages to accuse him. It makes a considerable crowd who will speak at his trial. Tomorrow every family must attend a ' people's trial ' which the police plan to make a model for villages accusing a former official. I'm afraid the news is very bad. They may even give him the death sentence."

Ling Ning had no trouble finding the abbot when she came out of the alley that ran between the hospital and the city wall. One urchin of five or six called to another, " Let's buy persimmons from Old Baldhead." The purchases were made and the boys ran off. While Ling Ning endlessly chose and rejected persimmons from his stock, the abbot told her what she had already heard from Lu Min. Over and over she interrupted him to express her appreciation for his really self-sacrificing effort on behalf of her uncle.

She told him of her mother's letter and of her frustrating helplessness.

" If I can get a word with your uncle," the abbot said, " the one message I shall give him besides trying to make him feel my own loyal friendship will be that your thoughts are with him."

"And that, no matter what the outcome, I'm not ashamed of him, or his record either! It's not shame that keeps me from going to him, but fear."

"If I can get the chance to speak a few words to him, they'll be comforting words. The difficulty is to get the chance. The trial is tomorrow, and it's altogether possible that if they decide on the death sentence, which I fear, they may carry it out at once. Death sentences can be deferred to see if a period of hard labor effects any reform. But in his case there's no hope of any such substitution. He wouldn't have the physical strength to do 'hard labor.'"

"What else have you heard about the accusation meeting? Is he the only one accused?"

"There is one other, but he is quite unimportant, and is sure to be let off with a jail sentence. The notice is going around that only one from each household may stay at home tomorrow. I wouldn't be surprised if the schools are to attend too. It's a big affair, the biggest Wangshan has had since the Liberation."

"The whole school? Oh, I couldn't bear to go. I'd be sure to break down entirely."

"Then you'd better get sick in the night," the abbot said. "I'm not sure that isn't the best thing for you to do anyway — then you can cry if you have to without arousing suspicion. One thing more — did you as a little girl have any nickname your uncle would recognize so that I could speak of you without using your name?"

Ling Ning answered eagerly: "I certainly did. My mother's brothers — and nobody else — called me 'Only Precious.' That was because my mother called me 'Precious' and I was the only one she had. That name would be absolutely safe, and at the same time carry a little hint of family affection. That's a good idea."

A customer interrupted the conversation, but Ling Ning waited for one more word. " I think I'll act upon your suggestion of the illness, but I ought to recover so I'll be able to come over here tomorrow at this time. Oh, if there were only something I could do for him! "

The abbot shook his head sadly. " There's no way! "

By putting some pepper on her handkerchief before she went to the evening study period, Ling Ning managed to sneeze at will, and finally excused herself. " If I'm coming down with a cold, this is the very worst time for giving it to others. Perhaps I'd better shut my sneezings up in my room."

She had told her intention to Lu Min and departed amid the solicitous murmurs of her colleagues. She stuck her head into Granny Mi's room and sneezed for her a few times, while she reported that it looked as though she might want her breakfast in bed the next morning. She was not amused by her own play-acting.

Awakened as usual by the rising bell, she pictured the routine activities as they were suggested to her by the sounds from the other courts. When Granny Mi came in, she sent her with a note to Principal Wang, asking to be excused from the morning's classes, with the added remark that, since it was Saturday, she hoped there was no essential duty for her in the afternoon either. Nothing had been said the evening before about an accusation meeting.

She heard the bell ring for the flag-raising, and then the shouted rendition of the national anthem. Only a minute later there was a great hubbub, with clapping of hands and squeals of pleasure, then running back and forth in the dormitory court.

In the midst of the hullabaloo, Granny Mi came close and whispered: " There aren't any classes. They're all going to the accusation meeting in the city at nine o'clock, and they're all tickled at the prospect; they think it's exciting, but it's too bad! The man who's being accused was the official here a few years ago. Everybody thought then that he was a good man. I hear that he didn't join the new Government and change his thoughts. It's harder for those of us who are older." She sighed, and asked what she could do for Ling Ning.

When Granny Mi and the students had gone, Ling Ning got up and dressed. She tried to check notebooks that were piled up on her desk, but could not keep her mind on them. She would find herself sitting staring at nothing, while her imagination painted the scene in the city.

The hours were long, and yet all too short if for her uncle they were the last ones. Finally she got out paper and pen and wrote a long letter to her mother. She told what she had learned from the abbot, and of her own successful avoidance of attending the accusation meeting. As she wrote, the tears came, and she made no effort to control them.

The girls returned noisily about half past three, but none came back to the Side Court and Ling Ning could tell that they were in high spirits only by the tones of their voices and by the snatches of song to which she knew they were dancing.

At last it was five o'clock and she might hope to find the abbot by the hospital. He was not at the appointed place. She took her letter to the postbox herself, then loitered back, stopping to look at the wares of every small merchant along the way, glancing often at the place where the abbot would meet her.

"Are you better?" someone asked beside her. Turning she found three of her third-year students with their book bags, day pupils on their way home. They did not wait for an answer, but gushingly commiserated with her upon having been sick on such a day.

"Everybody was there!"

"It was to condemn a bad old man who enriched himself by stealing from the people."

"We couldn't hear much, and we never did get near enough to see the man, but we all shouted whenever it was time: 'Ought to die! Ought to die!' Our People's Government will kill all those bad robbers."

"He took money away from the masses and bought an automobile to ride while everyone else walked. He was bureaucratic feudalism."

Her kindly uncle, with his plans for good roads for the farmers, and education for all the citizens, was the "bad old man" they talked about.

"Do you think, then, that our People's Government can kill everybody who in the past has taken the money of the people?" she asked.

"He ought to have changed his thinking. Perhaps then we could let him live." The girls went merrily on their way.

Ling Ning knew she was missing her supper, so she bought three *shao ping* — sesame-covered buns — and put them into her pocket. At school it was considered extravagant to buy extra things to eat, and she did not want to be seen doing it. At last, far away, she saw the dejected droop of the abbot's shoulders as he approached, pushing his wheelbarrow. His face had none of its usual animation.

"It's all over," he told her reluctantly, shaking his head. "He never had a chance."

Tears came into Ling Ning's eyes.

"They're already pasting up the posters announcing his

execution. Perhaps it was better not to have the mental torment of waiting, once the decision was made. He didn't have any time to think about it. With the shouts of the crowd, ' Ought to die! ' in his ears, he was hustled along in the middle of a little group of guards, through the main street, and out to the execution grounds. The students went home, but a big crowd followed, and I kept as near in front of it as I could. I hope he was so benumbed by all that had gone before that he felt nothing."

" And you never got to speak to him, did you? "

" Oh, yes, I did! " The abbot's eyes brightened. " It's odd how occasionally one runs into something that can't be done, and then finds it's not impossible at all. I had thought and thought and failed to find a way. And then I just went and did it as though they had told me to! "

Ling Ning listened, intent to hear how it could have been accomplished.

" I left my wheelbarrow at a shop and squeezed up to the very front of the crowd at the accusation meeting. I was quite near him, perhaps ten feet away. He didn't look up as he knelt for hours, listening to false accusations against him. There was a moment when the chairman and the leading accusers talked to each other, and I saw my chance. I crouched down and moved perhaps four or five feet closer, and said, ' I'm here! ' Your uncle looked at me, and if I did indeed put myself in danger by speaking to him, the look in his face was more than worth it. It meant that much to him to see a friend! I said, ' Only Precious says to tell you she is thinking of you with pride.' I could see he feared you were there, so while the guard was pushing me back, I said in a loud voice, ' She's not here! ' and I know he heard me. It was the last message he had from one he loved, and just about the last thing he ever heard."

Ling Ning had covered her trembling lips with her handkerchief.

" Your uncle kept himself calm through all those hours of speeches vilifying him. You must write and tell your mother."

" I'll tell her, and she'll pass the news on to my uncles and my cousins. Every one of them will be grateful to you.

" And — and do they bury such a criminal? " Ling Ning asked.

" They shoveled some dirt over him. I took careful note and can find the place. No one could conceive that anyone would dare to go to that execution ground and dig up a corpse. But I am going to do it tonight and take his body on this wheelbarrow out to the Temple of the Blue Lake. I have it all planned. I'll bury him on the east side of the entrance, outside the first tree in that avenue of pines. I'll put a small stone. It won't have any name on it, but if you ever want to find it, you'll have no difficulty, because I'll cut into the stone, as best I can, 'The Uncle of Only Precious.' The day might come when all this is forgotten and you could take him back to your family burying ground, but if that can never happen, I think he could rest at peace by that temple he loved."

" I think so too," Ling Ning assured him. " But a coffin! " That ought not be the abbot's responsibility. She knew he had no money for one. Besides, which of her uncle's family had done anything for him, as this good friend had done? She always carried in her inner pocket all the money she had, rather than leave it in her room. She took it out now and handed it to the abbot. " It won't be a good coffin, but that's all I have."

The abbot took the money and stuffed it into his pocket

without counting it. " I may not see you often, but you are always welcome at the — food stand. I was going to say the Temple of the Blue Lake. I've said it for many years, and all this about your uncle has brought back those days. What about you? Will you continue to teach here? Or will you perhaps marry that young man, Lu Min? "

" Oh, no! We just teach science in the same school. I've known him only since this term of school. There's never been a thought of marrying him."

" If there's never been one, there might well be. Forgive an old man for giving advice. I haven't seen him very often, but I judge that he'd make a good husband."

" I suppose Lu Min would make a good husband," Ling Ning agreed. On her mother's account she had not planned to marry young. She prepared to leave, first expressing her hope that the abbot would be successful in what he planned.

" Burn some incense for me," the abbot said. " The thing has some peril."

What he was planning to do was really dangerous. He would be constantly in her thoughts tonight. " I'll pray for you," she said, " but I won't burn any incense. I won't need to." Ling Ning was surprised at herself. She was planning to pray to the God Lu Min talked about, and she was sure he would hear her without the incense.

The next day Ling Ning got a note by Granny Mi from Lu Min.

" I think you need some sunshine. I've hunted up Nurse Sun and Timmy Tan and we'll start at one, as we did before, for another ride. I think we won't go toward the hills this time. Timmy knows another place. I'll borrow a wheel for you."

The abbot's suggestion that Ling Ning might well think of marrying Lu Min made her a little self-conscious when she met him at one o'clock. As soon as Nurse Sun and Timmy Tan joined the party she forgot all about it, and returned to her contented comradeship.

They went south this time again on one of the auto roads. Like the other, it was filled with travelers coming and going. The harvests had all been gathered, and the fallen leaves raked up and carried home for fuel. The earth lay bare under the winter sun. It was cold, but there was no wind, and the exercise was sufficient to keep them warm. Ling Ning's thoughts often went to the abbot and she wondered how he was faring. She felt sure that if the task could be carried out, he would accomplish it.

Timmy Tan, who often went about the countryside in his work as agricultural expert, had chosen their destination well. It was not a temple, but a large cemetery surrounded by a brick wall and entered through a gatehouse that was like a temple. Inside was a beautiful park, laid out in avenues that led to the larger graves. The trees were ancient pines, a soft, dull green. For a little tip, the gateman furnished tea. Timmy Tan had brought in a basket on his bicycle salty crullers, malt candy, and peanuts. The four of them sat on the carpet of pine needles and ate their lunch.

The cheerful fellowship was soothing. It had been wise of Lu Min to bring these two friends who knew nothing of Ling Ning's trouble, and who chatted about other things. After a while Ling Ning felt Lu Min watching her and, when she looked at him, caught an unspoken question. She nodded her head and smiled back. She felt as though she had been through a storm, but had weathered it. It had not overwhelmed her, but she knew it had changed her.

Timmy Tan and Lu Min kept a lively conversation going. They enjoyed each other and never had enough time together. Nurse Sun, though not of a taciturn nature, put in a sentence only now and then. Ling Ning, naturally quiet, listened with keen enjoyment.

Nothing was said about the events of the preceding day, but later Lu Min introduced the subject of forgiveness, and expressed the opinion that a person must be prepared to forgive without limit. He said that was what Jesus meant by "seventy times seven," and every Christian was in duty bound to forgive everything unceasingly and habitually, without considering a possible alternative.

Timmy Tan agreed with him. "A man in America wrote a novel about that general idea, that hatred and vindictiveness are like a poison in one's system. It's an interesting story, and I thoroughly believe the theme of it. But I wouldn't limit it to Christians. It's not just a Christian whose life can be soured and blighted by harboring something that remains unforgiven. Every human being has the same necessity to purge himself of such poison."

Ling Ning asked, "Do you mean that however unjust a thing is, one has to forgive the offenders?"

"That's right — not only for their sakes, but for one's own," Timmy Tan answered.

"It can't be done," Ling Ning said, half to herself. "It's not in human nature." Could she ever forgive those who had brought about the execution of her uncle, knowing as she did that the charges were untrue?

Again Timmy Tan answered: "I didn't say it was the human thing, the natural reaction of a man. You know how Jesus forgave those who had nailed him to the cross and, while hanging there suffering, prayed for them. That's one of the reasons why people worship him as more than human — as divine."

Ling Ning said no more. This was clearly a matter on

which the other three had thought more than she had. Even if they convinced her of their theory, she was sure she could not practice it. Not yet!

In the days that followed Ling Ning, thinking often of her uncle's family in their sorrow, noticed that she did not feel so deeply the persecutions she had to endure from the Youth League in the classroom. Other people had greater troubles!

Chapter 7

One of the joys of life under the People's Government was the fact that there was always a "meeting" either being held or being prepared for. One "little group" or another could always be found in one of the courtyards practicing a play or a dance. Every day the school's original waist-drum corps of eighteen older girls practiced new steps for an hour or so. Two more groups, eighteen each, of the younger girls were learning to beat the waist drums. All day long their rhythmic hubbub came from one court or another and recitation could barely be carried on. It was all patriotic activity, however, therefore came before lessons.

Sometimes the girls went to the boys' auditorium for moving pictures of the fighting in Korea. Often a program consisted of their own performances preceded by the energetic singing of all the patriotic songs they knew. There were always periods of shouted slogans; the leader never failed to call for "Resist America! Aid Korea!" "Ten thousand years to Chairman Mao!" and "Down with American imperialism!" The girls would sit through three or four or even five hours of this.

For December the Government announced a drive to enroll volunteers for the fighting in Korea, and one day in the first week of the month the Wangshan Girls' School held the meeting at which the necessary enthusiasm started. On such occasions it had been customary to ask Miss Pu to prepare a piano solo, since she could play the new patriotic songs as most of the people played the piano — the tune in the right hand while the left kept the time by drumming on some key or other that was not too far out of harmony. At this meeting Miss Pu played one of the most recent of their songs which ended, "Beat down America's wild wolf heart." The audience clapped enthusiastically when she had finished.

All would have been well if the meeting could have ended with the program as prepared. But at all such meetings, before the close there was a time for "as you please," which included the privilege of calling for some individual to perform. A few funny stories had been demanded and told, when a voice called, "A piano solo by Miss Ling." There was an instantaneous riotous clapping, which continued until Ling Ning arose.

"I didn't bring any music," she said, "and I have none suitable anyway."

The girls yelled and clapped, demanding anything she knew how to play, regardless of whether she thought it suitable. Remembering what had been said in the faculty criticism meeting, she shook her head. The noise became unbearable. Finally she looked at the principal, who nodded for her to go ahead.

It had occurred to her that she did know one piece that might do. When she went to the piano, she said diffidently, "I really don't know anything suitable and I really don't play without music, but it happens I know a sort of little parlor trick that's supposed to be funny."

"Play it! Play it!" the girls shouted.

"It's about chopsticks," she explained, "and maybe you

can imagine how fast someone is making them work." She sat down and played with all the speed she could command the clattering tune that, as a duet, has cheered so many pairs of young piano pupils.

At the end she turned to face a roomful of laughing girls. "Play it again! Play it again!" they shouted. It was the first time they had heard it, and they were enchanted.

She played it a second time, and then a third.

Then Miss Pu stood up, her face red and angry. The pandemonium ceased abruptly.

"What kind of music is that!" she exclaimed. "Why didn't you clap that way for patriotic music? Miss Ling is trying to show how much better she can play than I can. She's trying to make fun of me. But I'd rather play poorly something that will resist America and aid Korea, than play reactionary music the way she can."

Into a sullen silence the chairman announced, "The meeting is closed."

As the girls went out, some of them grinned slyly at Ling Ning. They had been pleased and amused with what she had played and, despite Miss Pu, persisted in thinking it had been fun. But Ling Ning was sorry she had done it.

At the next faculty study hour, while they were waiting for the meeting to begin, Ling Ning told Mr. Chen how troubled she was at the open break with Miss Pu in the presence of the students.

"She's jealous," he said. "If the girls hadn't clapped and laughed so, it would have been all right. She can't stand having anybody preferred over her. That's why they say she's going to get Principal Wang kicked out. He's too well liked."

"The principal!" Ling Ning was shocked. "I think of him as just perfect. Where would they get another so good? "

"From the Revolutionary College where she came from. But wait till she tackles you about Lu Min!"

"What do you mean 'about Lu Min'?"

"She was trying to catch his eye and thought she was getting along all right. You know how nice he is to everybody. And then you came along, and she can't even imagine he pays any attention to her now."

"I didn't know they were friends. Anyway, I haven't done anything but take a lot of help I don't know how I'd have got along without."

"What she'd have done with him if she'd had him is beyond me. He's too much of a Christian. Maybe she thought she could reform him. The only thing I'm sure of is that she hates you for spoiling her plans. I think she'll take it up with you. She's used to getting what she wants."

"Let her get him then," Ling Ning retorted in a whisper. The study hour was beginning.

She watched Miss Pu over in the opposite corner of the room and wondered if what Mr. Chen had just told her was true. What could Miss Pu and Lu Min have in common? Did he know she had such ideas about him? What did he think of it? And most of all, was it anything to her, Ling Ning?

One day in mid-December the gateman handed her a bit of paper. "A young man on a donkey brought it and said there was no answer, that you'd know who sent it. I can't make anything out of it."

The message was not even folded. It was brief.

"Only precious – plan completely accomplished – blue lake."

Ling Ning was well satisfied with what she read.

Ever since the Liberation the Government had increasingly controlled school activities. In the late fall, management of the Catholic University Fu Jen — the one from which Mr. Yang had graduated — had been taken over by the People's Government. That event had been sent out as a subject for discussion in all small groups. Hours had been spent in reading intensively the newspaper reports and expressing opinions. Each group invariably came to the conclusion that the Government had been quite right in ending the imperialism and feudalism practiced in that university, and in freeing the students for a life of new democracy.

So it was not a cause for surprise when one day the newspaper announced that the Government was taking over all mission schools. This would include Wangshan. The girls acted as if they were deliriously happy over undreamed-of good fortune. They threw their arms around each other and cried: " Truly free! Free at last! " It was no secret that they had been prepared in advance to make such a demonstration. So far as the daily schedule of life in the school was concerned, there was no change.

It was a long time since Ling Ning had had a call from the Wang sisters, but one evening they came secretly after study hall.

Tientsin said: " We don't know what to do. In our small groups the other girls say we have to sign up to go to Korea to fight. We told them we just couldn't."

" You'll have to tell me more about it," Ling Ning said. " Remember, I don't hear what goes on in your small groups."

" It's like this: They say every girl in our school ought to apply to go into the Army. Only twenty will be selected, so few of all who sign will be chosen. But the girls say that if a girl had even a little bit of patriotism she'd be willing to put her name down. Then our school could get the credit of being one hundred per cent patriotic."

"But," Little Sister interrupted, "both of us are going to be nurses someday. We have to graduate from junior high school first, so we have to stay here and study. We can't go off into the Army. I told the girls in my group how we've planned this ever since we were children, and that our parents are counting on us. They say not to tell our parents, but sign up, and then if we have to go, just go, and not tell them till afterward. I couldn't do that to my parents. Could you, Miss Ling?"

Miss Ling thought of her own mother. "No, I don't think I could."

"So they say, 'All right, then, ask your parents,'" Little Sister continued, "but I don't need to ask them. We've talked about it so much. I told the girls I knew my mother would never let me go, and they said, 'What would China come to if there were many such bad old women?' My mother is a good Christian woman. Everybody loves her. She only wants us to be nurses because she thinks that's such a good way to serve. The girls said if she didn't live so far away they'd go themselves and tell her what a selfish old woman she is." Little Sister's eyes filled with tears.

"In my small group they're even worse," Tientsin said. "They say that if I won't apply to join the Army, they'll see that I don't get free tuition."

"You're not getting it anyway," Ling Ning reminded her.

"No, not this term, but we've got to get it if we can. They say why be so scared when I'm sure not to have to go."

"If we really can't get free tuition, and have to stop school on that account, we might as well sign up," Little Sister pondered aloud. "They say there's another reason why we won't get free tuition. Do you remember I told you that Miss Pu and Mr. Chang put down our names that day at church? There have been students there to do it for them every Sunday since. Every girl who's been to church got only sixty in politics — just exactly passing — no matter what her recitations had been like. I'd got ninety-seven in my exam, and I got just sixty on my grade card. They say it's going to be the rule that you can't get free tuition unless your politics grade is eighty or more. It looks as though we wouldn't get the aid, but even so — "

"Has everybody else signed?" Ling Ning inquired.

Tientsin answered, "In our class there are twelve who haven't, but in my small group I'm the only one."

"In our class there are lots of day pupils," Little Sister said, "and some of them are just staying at home until the month's drive is over. Most of the boarders have signed." Then she added dolefully, "But I just can't."

"I can see your difficulty," Ling Ning finally told them. "But I don't think you ought to ask me for advice. Don't you see that the only thing I can say is to sign, since the Government has asked it?"

"But you haven't signed yourself," Tientsin pointed out.

"Don't let that decide you. Everyone must make her own decision." She wished she had some way to help them. "I had a teacher once who used to say, 'Imagine you're fifty years old, looking back, and decide everything the way you'll wish you had decided it.' If you used that rule, would you know what to do?"

They thought a few minutes.

"Yes," Tientsin said quietly. "I know the answer now. Looking back at it, a person wouldn't be so excited as we are. She'd say to me: 'If you wanted to be a nurse, why didn't you go ahead and be a nurse? Why did you let your classmates decide for you a thing that's so important as your lifework?' I'm not going to sign, no matter what they say. There are some who really want to go, and there are a lot more who don't want to go any more than I do. They're afraid not to sign, so they're pretending it's because they're so patriotic. That's not true patriotism. No, I'm not going to sign."

Little Sister was ready with her answer. "Fifty years old? That's about how old my grandmother is. I know what she'd say. She'd say: 'You're only thirteen. You don't know how to do anything well except study books, so you'd better do that with all your might until you're older. Go ahead and plan to be a nurse, and let the grownups run the war.'"

They were plainly relieved to have their minds made up, and went off with much happier faces.

The Wang girls were not the only ones who were disturbed by the necessity of deciding whether they should apply to go into the Army. It was always spoken of as volunteering to go to Korea, but the newspaper announcements of the drive said clearly that the young people who were chosen would enter training schools, without any promise of what their future would be. They were permitted in their applications to choose whether they preferred the Army, the Navy, or the Air Force.

Practically all the Wangshan girls were writing, "Air Force," and pictured themselves as pilots shooting down the wicked American planes that continually bombed the villages in China's northeast provinces.

There were only a handful who had not applied, and the pressure on them increased day by day. In class they sat inattentive, pondering. They rose and publicly asked Ling Ning for advice. The only thing she could say was that since the Government had sent out the notice, it was obvious that they expected patriotic young people to apply. Like Tientsin, they remarked aloud that Ling Ning herself had not applied.

Empress asked her in class whether she had ever applied for membership in the Youth League, and seemed to expect to discuss the matter then and there. It was useless to complain that these problems had nothing to do with the lessons and that they were far behind schedule. Nobody cared about the lessons, but everybody cared a great deal about these other questions.

They talked of nothing else all day, and held meetings half the night. A few of the leaders of the Youth League had set as a goal, " Everybody must apply," and they had worked themselves to a nervous frenzy which they thought of as patriotic zeal.

Each watched the others. On one occasion, as she entered the teachers' room, Ling Ning saw one of the older girls leaving by the farther door. When she reached her desk, she found on it a letter from her mother that had been opened and resealed. The gateman, when taxed with this information, confessed that the girls were taking all her mail as soon as the postman brought it — " to inspect it," they said. Ling Ning was glad that she had long since warned her mother, and that she received few letters from other people.

Ling Ning was relieved that, after denouncing her publicly, Miss Pu again ignored her. She had enough trouble trying to pacify the excited students without having the necessity of conciliating Miss Pu.

Ling Ning never spent any time analyzing her feeling toward the older teacher. She never misdoubted the dislike she had carried over from her childhood. On the contrary, she had rather taken for granted that all normal people would look upon Miss Pu as she did. She did not exactly hate the woman. Her dislike was a mixture of contempt and fear. As a child her strategy had always been to retreat, to avoid the bigger girl's unpleasantness. Now her fear was augmented by the power of Miss Pu's position. Ling Ning was still no fighter. Her reaction, as in childhood, was to shun rather than challenge. She was well pleased that Miss Pu wanted nothing to do with her.

One morning in late December, when Ling Ning went to the teachers' room for her vacant period, the one in which she and Lu Min so often compared notes, she found Miss Pu sitting in her chair at her desk, looking very unhappy. Engrossed in what she was saying to Lu Min, she had not seen Ling Ning coming, but hearing the door close, she turned. " I suppose you'd like to sit here," she said tartly.

" It's of no importance," Ling Ning answered, preparing to go to one of the many vacant desks nearby.

" I'm afraid that won't be so convenient for your little chat with your boy friend," Miss Pu sneered, not offering to move. " The girls say you're even reading the Bible with him. Imagine that! "

Ling Ning was taken aback. Little as she liked an argument, she was sufficiently irritated to retort, " And if I did, I don't know any reason why you should call me to account for it."

" Oh, you don't! Lu Min is always talking of religious liberty. That doesn't mean liberty to proselyte, nor to bring Bibles into a school. But that's not the only interesting thing I've been hearing about you. There's this story Lu Min's been telling me about your uncle."

" My uncle! " Ling Ning was aghast.

" That reactionary Official Wang who was executed a few weeks ago! And you thought you'd kept it so secret."

Ling Ning gazed in horror at Lu Min. He did not look

up, but said, " I haven't told her anything."

Sick at heart, Ling Ning accused him, " You — you traitor! "

" He's not so nice as you thought, is he! " Miss Pu taunted. " Wait till the girls hear about this. A reactionary niece to a reactionary uncle. After what he got, don't you think it's time for you to change your thoughts? "

" I'm not reactionary," Ling Ning stated flatly. Constant reports of Government action against " reactionary elements " had made the word sinister. Ling Ning could not allow it to pass unchallenged.

" That's what your uncle said," Miss Pu retorted. " He claimed that he had tried to serve the people. I suppose the first thing we know you'll be claiming that in teaching here you are serving the people."

" I certainly do claim that," Ling Ning asserted stoutly. " If you're serving the people by teaching here, so am I."

" How perfectly impossible you are! You can't serve the people so long as your thoughts are wrong, your attitude wrong, your point of view wrong. You're capitalist through and through. All my Youth League girls know it, without having caught you at anything. But this uncle of yours! " She laughed triumphantly. " I don't know how I happened not to think of it. I remember — I mean — "

" You remember that my mother's brothers were named Wang, and that one of them, who sometimes came to our house, was an official. You'd seen him many times, but failed to recognize him here because you failed to put two and two together."

" Will you stop that crazy raving! I never heard of you, or your uncles, or your mother's family, or your house on Kan Mien Hutung — "

" How did you know it was on Kan Mien Hutung? "

Miss Pu stammered with rage. " Tell as many lies as you like. See if anybody will believe you. Your uncle's niece ought to be able to get quite a following. But don't forget I can call on my Youth League girls."

Into Ling Ning's mind flashed memories of all that had happened in her classroom within recent weeks. Now it was going to be unspeakably worse. She looked at Lu Min. He was still sitting in a dejected fashion, his pencil drawing squares and circles on a piece of paper. He did not look up. Ling Ning glanced at the gloating Miss Pu, and knew herself defeated.

" If you'll excuse me," she said weakly, and left the room.

She went back to the Side Court and sat in a daze until the bell rang. Having prepared her lessons carefully, she went through her classes like an automaton. Not even her uncle's death had so overwhelmed her. Why had Lu Min betrayed her? How had he had the heart to? Was she really in danger of being unjustly accused as her uncle had been?

Chapter 8

It remained beautiful weather, still cold, with a warm sun and no wind. Everybody had long since put on padded clothes. Ling Ning had had the tailor's shop make hers out of her last year's long padded coat, the style being like her summer clothes, a Russian blouse tied at the waist, with awkward bulky trousers. Dressed thus, with her black padded shoes and the blue mittens she had worn at Yenching, she was warm in the draftiest classroom. She did not even have chilblains as most of the students did. She was unhappy, but her discomfort was not physical.

School life was, if anything, busier. It was near enough to the end of the term for the office to have sent out word to begin reviewing for final examinations. The students had done so little studying that review was imperative, and yet there was not enough time to go over all the term's work. A compromise was effected: the teachers made long lists of questions from which they would choose those in the examinations. Ling Ning worked hard preparing her list, inexperienced as she was in giving term finals. Then daily she helped the students copy the right answer to each question from their books or notes, ready to cram at the last minute. She worked much harder than they did, and without the hope of attaining very good results. Empress actually suggested that she might as well just say right out which questions she planned to ask. There were many supporters of this idea, but Ling Ning refused to consider it.

The twenty girls who were to be permitted to represent the school in aiding Korea had been selected. The announcement was made at assembly, and as soon as it was over, their classmates carried the future heroes through all the courts on their shoulders — something they had seen done in moving pictures. They shouted and laughed, and yelled slogans. The waist-drum corps added enormously to the pandemonium. No one knew the reactions of the girls who were chosen, beyond what they said — that it was an honor beyond their hopes. But it was known that a number of students had been tense with fear that they would be chosen, and were now hysterical with delight that their names had been passed. The pupils who had been staying at home on sick leave returned. In the end there were forty-three who had not applied to go, to the great disgust of Empress and her friends.

Ling Ning did her part in all the celebrations. Invited to play a piano solo at one of the farewell meetings, she ascertained that Miss Pu was going to play the newest of the patriotic pieces, a long one somewhat in the old Chinese style. Then she laboriously wrote out for herself the music of her favorite, the one with the phrase "China's good sons and daughters," which kept going through her head. Though she had never studied harmony, she made an accompaniment to play with her left hand, and practiced it until she could do it quite smoothly. The final concoction, while appreciably superior to Miss Pu's way of drumming, was not worth the time and energy spent on it, but she determined that she would not again be criticized for the kind of music she played.

Ling Ning was glad to be so busy. Even without a minute of leisure in which to think, she was so unhappy that she could hardly endure it. She could not have been made to believe that losing the companionship of Lu Min would make her feel so forsaken. It was not that she did not see him. His desk was still next to hers, and at morning and evening faculty study hours they sat near each other and took part in the discussion. They still ate at the same dining table. But since that horrid morning when Ling Ning had learned of his treachery, she had never looked at him or acted as though he were there. She intended to ignore him for the rest of her life.

Angry and hurt, she could refuse to look at him or speak to him, but she could not stop thinking of him. She would set her mind to something else. Yet very soon she would be reviewing Lu Min's part in her uncle's trouble. It had been Lu Min who had been sure it must be kept secret. He had been unwilling that Nurse Sun or Timmy Tan, his best friends, should be told anything at all for fear they might inadvertently give a hint that might harm her. Why then, after her uncle had been publicly branded as a reactionary, had he told the secret to the one person who was most likely to use it to make the most trouble? Over and over it went through her mind. She found no way out of the maze.

At another time she decided that the only way to understand Lu Min was to revamp her whole conception of his character. Obviously he was not the sort of man she had thought. She was too inexperienced, and had accepted him as he appeared, courteous, brainy, diligent, considerate. How considerate she had thought him! Clearly she had been deceived by his pleasant manners. Otherwise, there was no explanation.

He was a Christian, too. And yet he had lied to her. " I

haven't told her anything," he had said, denying that Miss Pu had learned from him what only he knew. Ling Ning did not stop to think that she was holding a higher standard for Lu Min than she did for anybody else. Nowadays everybody lied. The girls did not believe each other. They demanded that they see with their own eyes or hear with their own ears, and even then they sometimes questioned whether what they saw and heard was not false. Ling Ning was not shocked when other people told lies, but Lu Min was a Christian.

Miss Pu had repeatedly warned him that she planned to make trouble for him unless he recanted. That morning he had looked very uncomfortable. Was it because he had bought off Miss Pu with information that he knew she would jump at? That wasn't like Lu Min. None of it was like the Lu Min Ling Ning had thought she knew.

That was the Lu Min she was lonely for!

Meanwhile, she was more afraid of Miss Pu than ever. And Miss Pu knew it. Whenever the two met, she wore an enigmatic, teasing smile, gloating. She was like a cat playing with a mouse.

Gladly now Ling Ning would have told the story she had suppressed when she first came to Wangshan, but she knew that nobody in the Girls' School would believe it. The telling would only put her farther in the wrong herself. She was helpless.

Ling Ning broke her habit of going every afternoon for a few minutes' chat with Nurse Sun. Her excuse, that she was too busy, was plausible. She was afraid Nurse Sun, seeing her so distraught, would ask questions. Being restless, she went out on the big street to divert her thoughts. Often the day pupils passed her there as they hurried home to their suppers, and gave her friendly smiles. Met so, as individuals, they were always agreeable, not truculent and rude as they often were in class. She treasured these pleasant contacts.

One day it was Tientsin whom she met. " I've been to the post office," the girl explained. She stopped and seemed to want to talk. " My father sent the money for our fare home and I went to get the order cashed. My! I'm glad the money's come."

" There's plenty of time before the winter holidays."

" Not so long! Little Sister isn't coming back. I have to, because I can't transfer in the middle of my last year. By staying away from church, I'll be able to stick it out, but there's no reason why Little Sister should. She can go to a Government school in Tientsin that's just as good or better than this."

" Why didn't she in the first place? It seems odd to come all the way here."

" You see, this was a Christian school, but now it hasn't as much religious freedom as they have in the former Government schools. There the students are really free to believe as they please, the way our People's Government promised it would be for all of us. It's only one term — then I'll get into a nurses' school in Tientsin. I hear the course is cut from three years to two. It won't be long till I'm a nurse." She smiled proudly. " I'm glad I didn't decide to go into the Army. You helped me a lot to see that one has to think a long time ahead. Poor Fatty! You know that girl I'm always with, the one with the round face and the dimples? "

" Yes, I know. She's usually so jolly. And now she's been chosen to go to aid Korea."

" It's terribly sad. Empress and the other girls promised her she wouldn't be chosen, so she signed without telling her mother. Her mother's a widow who has sewed to put her through school and was just counting the days till Fatty would be through, and could maybe get a job, or into some Government vocational school where it would all be free and she'd soon have learned a skill of some kind. Fatty doesn't dare tell her, and she can hardly keep from crying all the time she's eating the farewell dinners."

Ling Ning could picture what it would mean to her own mother, and pitied both Fatty and the poor widow.

"Perhaps it won't be long until the fighting is over, and Fatty can come back and go on with her mother's plans for her," she suggested.

"Perhaps," Tientsin echoed doubtfully. "I'll miss her next term. And I'll miss Little Sister too, but she says the only reason she'd like to come back is to study with Miss Ling. She thinks you're wonderful. You've certainly been good to us."

The girl's sweet way and unconcealed affection were comforting.

The next time Ling Ning went to see Nurse Sun, she found her friend upset by the news Timmy Tan had brought her of Lu Min. At first she was surprised that Ling Ning knew nothing about it, supposing them to be as good friends as ever.

"No, I'm not surprised either," she said. "Lu Min doesn't talk about himself or his own affairs. I'll guarantee that as well as you know him you don't know that he's all alone in the world except for a married sister in Shansi. They weren't even brought up together. They were both boarders at mission schools, and stayed through vacations because they hadn't any place to go. This uncle's about all they had."

"And what about the uncle?"

"He's committed suicide."

"Oh! How sad! Why did he do it?"

"He's been one of the leading Christians in Shanghai,

and maybe you've noticed in the paper how they're accusing each other. He was given orders by the police to accuse one of his best friends of having cheated the church of money. Of course it was a lie. He wouldn't do it. This is his protest."

"When did Lu Min hear?"

"He got his uncle's farewell letter yesterday. Timmy says he's really sunk. He told Timmy that dying as a protest might not be worth the price — that living as a protest is just as hard, and probably more effective. But he doesn't blame his uncle. He thinks each individual must decide such matters for himself. Just the same, it makes him feel very lonely, as though the bottom had dropped out of things. He's always admired this uncle and known he could fall back on him in a pinch."

"Another uncle! What a coincidence!" Ling Ning thought, but she could not say it. She listened to Nurse Sun's regrets for the uncle and sympathy for Lu Min and knew that her own pity could have gone much deeper. From her own recent experiences she could understand how bereft he must feel. It was a time for friends to rally round, but it was nothing to her. She was no longer a friend of Lu Min's. Let Timmy Tan comfort him.

The day arrived for the departure of the twenty heroes who were joining the Army. One of the charcoal-burning buses came from Peking for them and the city Government of Wangshan gave a final feast. On the chest of each girl was pinned a huge red silk flower. Their fellow students cheered, and beat their waist drums. The girls climbed into the bus, and they were off.

"I suppose we shan't have any more excitement this term," Ling Ning remarked to Mr. Yang, who walked back to the teachers' room with her.

"I wouldn't be too sure," he said. "When people are

so worked up, they're likely to do almost anything. I've heard mutterings of thunder. And speaking of Lu Min – "

She wondered why he said, " Speaking of Lu Min," when they had not been speaking of him, but she did not interrupt.

" What's the matter with you two? "

" Ask him," was Ling Ning's answer.

" I did, and he said to ask you."

What did it matter? Since Miss Pu knew all she did, it was no longer a secret from anybody. Ling Ning took advantage of the quiet in the empty teachers' room to tell Mr. Yang the whole story. He chuckled when she told him about Miss Pu's childhood.

" Explains everything," he muttered, without really interrupting. He clucked in sympathy when she told him about her uncle. But when she told about the quarrel with Miss Pu and Lu Min's part in it, he shook his head.

" How could a girl go through a university and still be so dumb? " he asked.

Ling Ning was taken aback. Was he talking about her?

" You know, since you've come here, so pretty and attractive, I've sometimes imagined what it would be like to be married to a girl like you, instead of to the kind of wife I've got."

" What? You're married? "

" Yes, and have four children. That's the big reason I'm so anxious to keep my job."

" But where is she? "

" At home, out in the country with my parents. She's an uneducated country girl, and hasn't any of the things you have. One would have to be blinder than I am not to appreciate her ability as a housekeeper – getting over the days, making a little money go a long way; and she's a wonderful daughter-in-law to the old folks — I think I've always recognized that sometimes that sort of thing isn't as easy as it looks — and she's a good mother to my children. She's not bad-looking and keeps herself neat, and she's a good neighbor. Today I'm impressed by another of her virtues, and I'm not sure it isn't worth the lot. There's nobody on this earth could make her believe anything bad about me."

There was a little silence. Ling Ning wasn't quite sure what the implications were. She waited for Mr. Yang to go on.

"We've all been watching you and Lu Min, and thinking it was going to be a match, and a good one. And now it's off. I'll bet now if you took a notion you couldn't catch him. I think he's too smart to marry a girl who's going to believe every lie she hears about him."

"But it was he who told the lie. He said he'd never told Miss Pu anything. And he was the only person who knew anything about my uncle."

"You still don't catch on. Your mind's so made up. Look! If Pu and Lu Min told you two different stories about some ordinary thing like the price of corn, which would you believe?"

"Why — Lu Min."

"Sure! But on something important like this, you swallow her bait! I'll bet she's gloating."

In her imagination, Ling Ning saw Miss Pu's smile. Yes, she had gloated. "But — nobody knew except Lu Min."

"You can depend on it that the men who accused your uncle looked up not only his affairs but also those of his family as well. To them it was a comparatively uninteresting item that his niece was teaching in Wangshan, but when that information finally circulated around to Pu, she found it the choicest tidbit of all. And then she led you to believe Lu Min told her."

"She might not even have known he knew," Ling Ning said in amazement. "She could have been just guessing!"

"Yes."

"What must Lu Min think!"

"I know what I'd think if a girl did a trick like that to me."

The conversation was ended abruptly by the entrance of two other teachers, and after a few minutes Ling Ning got away to her own room.

The mistake had been hers, instead of Lu Min's! Mr. Yang's comments had not been flattering, but they had been both sincere and just.

Ling Ning mulled over the conversation. The mistake was hers. It was her business to rectify it. Mr. Yang had been sure Lu Min would be unwilling to have anything more to do with her, and Mr. Yang had a fairly high percentage for being right. Ling Ning did not like the idea of apologizing, but now that she was convinced that she was in the wrong, she could see no other way out of it. She would apologize right away.

At supper Lu Min came late. For the first time in several weeks Ling Ning looked at him. She was shocked at his appearance. How could he have become so thin in so short a time? His face was haggard. She had never seen him anything but courteous, and he was courteous now, in a negative sort of way, giving absent-minded monosyllabic answers when spoken to. He ate only one bowlful of millet porridge and excused himself. He had never once looked in her direction.

Ling Ning went early to evening study hour, to wait for Lu Min. He came late, and took his place with a preoccupied listlessness which ignored not only Ling Ning but the other teachers as well. She could not make an apology in study hour. She would speak to him the minute it was over.

They were studying a little booklet called *Handbook of Facts*, one in a series that had begun in October. The number they were studying gave the history of the long aggression of the United States against China, something about the liberation of Tibet, and a short article about MacArthur's policy. The evening's lesson was about the news from Korea. It was supplemented by the newspaper. The Chinese volunteers and the Northern Koreans were achieving great victories, pushing the invading Americans toward the southern tip of the country. Every day the reports had been so encouraging that the final success seemed near.

The study hour reflected the good news. Miss Pu was particularly gay. When the two-minute bell rang for the end of the session, she was laughing loudly at some joking remark of her friend, Mr. Chang.

What happened next was so rapid and confused that though she was right there in the midst of it, Ling Ning could not have reported it accurately. There was a guffaw of laughter around Miss Pu, and then she called, "Will you go to Korea, Lu Min?"

"No," he said, with no particular emphasis.

"Why not?" Miss Pu asked, still laughing.

"Why aren't you?" he answered.

She suddenly became sober. "I'm no lover of America," she said. It was an expression which had been for some time practically equivalent to reviling, since it was an accusation of a lack of patriotism.

He had lost all his lassitude. "You can't put that hat on me."

" It's already on you," she boasted.

" No more than on you, if you don't go," Lu Min retorted.

With lightning suddenness Miss Pu's mood changed to anger, anger that was awful in its intensity. She sputtered, " You dare say that to me! " and then, bursting into sobs, ran from the room, weeping loudly.

The room was full of questions.

" What did he say? "

" What made her so mad? "

" What happened, anyway? "

" Now she's got it," Mr. Yang said to Mr. Chen, who was on his way to the door.

" Who's got what? " Ling Ning asked.

" Pu. What she's been waiting for."

Ling Ning wanted to ask him what he meant, but he was leaving.

Lu Min was already at the door. Ling Ning heard Principal Wang say to him, anxiously, " Can't you fix that up some way? "

" I'll try."

By the time Ling Ning reached the courtyard, it was full of clamoring students and disturbed teachers. The loudest sounds were Miss Pu's crying and the voices of some of the older students trying to quiet her.

Chapter 9

Ling Ning spent a restless night. Lu Min was definitely in trouble. Mr. Yang and Mr. Chen had recognized that fact at once. The principal knew it. It was in his anxious " Can't you fix that up? " The gloom with which Lu Min answered, " I'll try," proclaimed it. Ling Ning could not guess what form the trouble might take, but she knew that she was deeply concerned.

It was no use trying to ascertain just what had so angered Miss Pu. The important thing was to conciliate her, and such a public exhibition of rage was not going to be appeased easily.

Meanwhile, now that this blow had fallen on Lu Min, Ling Ning was more conscious than ever of her own offense against him and of the necessity for acknowledgment of this to him.

At the morning study hour he did not appear. Neither did Miss Pu. No mention was made of either. In unexpressed tenseness the rest of the teachers went through the daily routine. They read the next article in their *Handbook of Facts* and discussed it for an hour.

At breakfast, with Lu Min's place vacant, Ling Ning heard some news.

" He's with the Student Union," one of the men said. " They met all night." Holding an all-night meeting was not an uncommon practice when something important was under consideration. Time had to be given to every member to express thoughts on the subject. An all-night meeting indicated that the present problem was deemed an important one.

The class schedule went on as usual. Ling Ning did not make any inquiry about all the empty seats, and no excuses were offered. The absentees were members of the Student Union.

At morning recess she noticed a large sheet of paper posted beside the wall newspaper. The characters on it were too small to be read from a distance. A crowd of girls surrounded it, and they were writing on it with their Chinese brush pens, only a few words, as though they were signing their names. She did not want to appear too curious about what was obviously a student affair, but she asked a little girl going by what the paper was.

" It's a petition to the Government educational department to send away Mr. Lu. It has all our names on it in pencil, and if we want to sign, we put our name in ink over the pencil one. That's so it's easy to tell when everybody has signed."

Two more students passed her. " I signed for you," one said.

" I — I wasn't going to," the other objected. " I like Mr. Lu."

" I was afraid of that. You'd get into a lot of trouble. Everybody has put her name down, no matter what she thinks of Mr. Lu. And you'd better not tell any of the Youth League girls you like him."

" I know it," the other conceded sadly.

From where she stood Ling Ning could see that most of the spaces were already black with Chinese ink. Poor Lu Min!

That afternoon she sought Nurse Sun and poured out all the secrets she had been so carefully guarding. Her own troubles which had seemed so overwhelming were all insignificant beside Lu Min's. Worst of all, in her mind, was the fact that she could do nothing to help him. She could not even give him the comfort — if comfort it should be — of letting him know she was sorry she had distrusted him. She had been so unreasonable and so rude!

"Do you suppose he'll ever forgive me?" she asked Nurse Sun, tearfully.

"Of course! He believes in forgiving. Besides, he's very fond of you. You surely know that."

"He's like that with everybody."

At that Nurse Sun laughed. But she was immediately sober again. "When I saw Lu Min on Sunday I thought he looked terrible. I didn't know about this misunderstanding with you, and supposed it was all due to his grief over his uncle. The poor fellow has more than his share of difficulties, and all at once."

"The teachers seem to think the quarrel with Miss Pu is serious."

"Worse than that! She'll run him out, and it won't take her long. I'd say today or tomorrow. Timmy had better get most of Lu Min's things out of his room. We'll see about that tonight and bring them over here so that nobody can get at them. You can't tell what those girls may do with Miss Pu egging them on to avenge whatever wrong she thinks has been done her."

"Pirate's a good man; he'll help," Ling Ning suggested. It was encouraging to be thinking of some activity that could conceivably be useful, instead of just fruitlessly worrying.

"And I think you'd better send your box over here, and anything else you can get along without."

"Me? Do you think — "

"I think she doesn't like you any better than she does Lu Min."

"Not so well," Ling Ning was sure.

"Likely as not, she'll fix it so you'll have to leave at the end of the term at the latest." Miss Sun broke off to ask abruptly, "How well do you like Lu Min?"

"Awfully well," Ling Ning answered.

"Then pull out when he goes, and if you can't find a chance to talk to him here you can talk to him in Peking."

It was a new idea to Ling Ning, but it was like the opening of a door before her. Her face lighted up with the possibilities she saw.

She and Nurse Sun talked faster than ever in the few minutes left before she had to hurry back to supper.

Supper without Lu Min — Was he getting anything to eat?

Ling Ning would have been beside herself with worry if she had not been so busy. She called in Granny Mi, but when she started to talk, she found that the old lady knew more about what was going on than she did. Granny Mi nodded at Ling Ning's report of Nurse Sun's fears for her.

"They say they'll have a criticism meeting for you as soon as they finish with him," the old woman reported. She approved Nurse Sun's suggestion that Ling Ning store her things at the hospital, preparatory to leaving with Lu Min. Their whispered conference was short and ended in prompt action.

The bedding had to wait till Ling Ning was through sleeping there. She pulled her big box out from under the bed and prepared to put into it almost all her other – not too numerous – possessions. She wanted to give Granny Mi a gift. She took out the " old-fashioned clothes " to look them over as possibilities. Oldest of all was a short jacket of black satin lined with fur. It had not been worn for years, but her mother, thinking of Wangshan as colder than Peking, had made her bring it. It was just the thing for an old woman and worth enough to be the sort of present Ling Ning wanted to give her.

The old lady was overwhelmed. She swore she would not accept so nice a gift, but beamed with delight when Ling Ning forced it on her.

"You mustn't let the girls know," Ling Ning reminded her.

Granny Mi needed no such reminder. She started to take it to her own room. "Tomorrow I'll leave it with a friend who lives over by the church. She'll keep it for me till these girls have graduated and there's a new batch." She giggled like a little girl in her pleasure.

After that Ling Ning's preparations went faster. There was danger that some girl might wander into the Side Court and discover her preparations to leave. Granny Mi kept watch until the box was packed. By half past ten Ling Ning's things were outside the gate in a ricksha on their way to the hospital. She could leave Wangshan now on very short notice.

When Ling Ning returned, she heard girls in the dormitory courts. The school was far from being as quiet as it usually was after the last bell. She was tired, but too tense to sleep. In the daytime, when she was talking with Nurse Sun, running away had appeared simple and easy. In the night, alone, it was full of possible miscalculations. If Miss Pu was in fact planning some action against her, and she were caught trying to avoid it, she would lose more face than if she had waited until the term was over — if Miss Pu would wait until the term was over! But there was Lu Min — Ling Ning couldn't let him go without knowing she was sorry. She couldn't let him go without her. How could she endure Wangshan if he were gone? And what was he doing now? Had they let him eat anything? They could take turns arguing with him while others went to rest, but had they given him any chance to sleep? Was the Student Union having another night session with him? If not, why was there so much running back and forth in the dormitory courts? Poor Lu Min!

A few minutes after the rising bell Ling Ning heard a light rap on her door. It was Pirate. "Mr. Tan says he'll come at your breakfast time to this side gate," he whispered.

Impatiently Ling Ning read with the other teachers the next article in the *Handbook of Facts,* and tried to think of something to say in the discussion. Timmy Tan was sure to have news about Lu Min's affairs, and they were much more interesting to her than the *Facts.* She hurried out the minute she could get away.

"I've failed to see Lu Min," Timmy Tan reported, "but that man Pirate is a godsend! We've taken all Lu Min's clothes and books and papers — everything but his bedding, almost. They're in the hospital gatehouse, ready to be taken to the bus whenever he goes. Gossip says it'll be today."

"I don't hear anything," Ling Ning complained, "until it's happening!"

" From what Pirate tells me, I think you'd better go today," Timmy Tan answered. " Most of your things are over there. I'll take everything else now, and all you'll have to do is walk out. I'll get a ricksha while you're gathering them together. Don't pack. Just dump all the little things in the middle of your comfort, and I can straighten them out over there. You might get caught at it here."

" Don't we have to get a change-of-residence permit from the police? " Ling Ning reminded him.

" I was coming to that. The girls have it all cooked up that they'll keep Lu Min here until time to leave, then escort him over to the bus. He'll have no chance to go to the police office for a transfer. Then as soon as he arrives in Peking he'll be in trouble with the police because he can't register his residence. They're smart girls, or else somebody is being smart for them. Lu Min has no offense here that the police would listen to, so they're making one for him the minute he gets to Peking."

Ling Ning was horrified. " It never would have occurred to me! But it could get him into a lot of trouble, couldn't it? "

" So it's up to us to get him a transfer." Timmy Tan took from his pocket some sheets of paper. " A transfer for a few days is very simple. You just get the local head man to stamp your application, and take it with your residence certificate and the police give you a permit. For permanent change of residence you must have four copies, and there's a little more red tape. What complicates this for you and Lu Min is that you haven't residence certificates. All you folks connected with the school are just registered together under the school and don't go through the local man. If you want to go anywhere permanently you have to have a certain school seal on your application —

a seal they have especially for this. I learned all this from Pirate. He often helps manage it for the girls. He's afraid to be involved in this affair of Lu Min's, and he's right. It would probably cost him his job. So it's up to you."

"I see – but – how could I do it?"

"I've written out the applications for you, four for you and four for Lu Min. When you go to the school office, say your mother needs you to come home at once to attend to some business. The man will say one application sheet is enough. And if you can help it he mustn't know that you're doing anything for Lu Min. I don't know how you're going to get that seal and use it eight times!"

Neither did Ling Ning. It appeared to her very unlikely that she could work any bluff on the man in the school office. He had always been friendly and pleasant, but he was exceedingly businesslike and was not likely to turn her loose in his office to do as she pleased. She would indeed say she had to go to Peking for a few days, but he would certainly object to her stamping eight pieces of paper.

"I have Lu Min's seal," Timmy was going on as though, having given her the hardest job of all, he saw it already accomplished. "Pirate got that. What would I have done without that man! I'll take it and go with you to the police office. We must get in there before twelve. With the bus leaving at two, we don't dare risk waiting till after the noon hour. It doesn't make any difference what you're doing. You'll have to pull out of it about eleven, get those papers stamped, and run over to the hospital back gatehouse. I'll be waiting for you there with bicycles, so that if you're pretty late, we can still be inside the police office by twelve. Doesn't that sound all right?"

It sounded too easy. Timmy Tan certainly had figured it all out. She was grateful to him.

"Now get your things ready. I'm going for a ricksha. I'll race you." He knew how worried and apprehensive she was.

She was really too late for breakfast, but the cook had not cleaned up yet and the millet gruel was cool enough to be eaten fast. With a big bowlful inside her, she was warmed and given courage.

At flag-raising it was announced that, instead of the regular classes, everybody should go at once to the assembly hall for a "big" criticism meeting. So that was what was ahead of Lu Min!

As in the case of other official events, the meeting was held with ceremony. Principal Wang presided. The faculty sat in the front seats on one side where they always sat, and the students were all present, as at every full assembly.

Lu Min was seated conspicuously toward the edge of the platform. He looked as though he had just got up from a serious illness. His face was sallow and drawn, thin and pale. He sat quite composed, just waiting for whatever they chose to do to him. Only his hands betrayed his nervousness, as he kept moving back and forth the pencil and notebook he held.

Opposite the teachers, in the other front corner, was a long table at which sat Empress and five or six other leading students. They too were equipped with pencils and paper, ready to take notes of the proceedings.

The principal opened the meeting. They all rose and sang "*Chi lai*," having sung it not more than ten minutes earlier at flag-raising in the courtyard. They also sang "Union Is Strength," and shouted slogans.

Then the principal stated that the purpose of the meeting was to criticize Lu Min, a teacher, for pro-American sympathies and lack of patriotism. Principal Wang also said that since the Liberation the Wangshan Girls' School had never held a "big" criticism meeting, and that he hoped they would follow the rules laid down by the Government for such meetings and make this one a model for themselves in the future. He reserved the right as chairman to hold them to the rules, which they had all studied but never practiced. There should be no quarreling or calling of names. He would insist on dignified behavior.

Then he made the opening speech. It was a report of the quarrel between Miss Pu and Lu Min at the faculty study hour. Ling Ning was interested to hear it told: it had been so confusing at the time. The principal told it as Ling Ning remembered it — how they had been laughing and joking, and then Miss Pu had asked Mr. Lu, "Will you go to Korea?" He answered, "No." "Why aren't you going?" she had asked. "Why aren't you?" he had answered. She had then said, "I'm no lover of America." "You can't put that hat on me." "It's already on you." The principal went on to say that the Student Union had had under consideration for several days this accusation against Mr. Lu and had decided that the whole school should make the decision as to what should now be done. The will of the masses should be final, and they were met to discover what that will was.

Ling Ning had always admired Principal Wang. It seemed to her that so far he had handled this quite fairly. He went on to announce that Mr. Lu would not answer each criticism as it was made but would take notes, and would be called on at intervals to answer several accusations together. The secretaries — he indicated Empress and her helpers — would also take full notes, both of the criticisms and of his answers. Each student was free to speak whatever she had to say. It was absolute democracy.

While the principal was talking Ling Ning, in looking about, noticed in the back of the room several of the young men teachers from the Boys' School whom she had met casually. She wondered what they were doing there. While they were quietly waiting for someone to speak, a representative of the Government educational department came in, one of the less important men. He was asked to speak, and replied that he would later. He sat down in the front of the room, along with the faculty.

Ling Ning was glad she was sitting next to Mr. Yang. She liked him and hated to think that after today she might never see him again. He also had a pencil and a pad of paper. Her own hands were empty. Perhaps if she had wanted to she could have found in one of the many pockets of her uniform something to write upon. She had filled them all with various small articles she might want to take away with her. She was conscious of none of them, but only of that pocket which held, safely folded, the eight applications on which she must get the school seal stamped before twelve o'clock. Would this meeting finish in time? She was doubtful. The man from the office was not present. She hoped he was keeping the office open. Would she have the courage to get up and leave, with the whole school looking at her? She looked at Lu Min, sitting there so patiently, and made up her mind that when the time came, even if she did not want to do it for herself, she would do it for him.

There had been a whispered conversation between one of the Boys' School teachers and a third-year girl whom Ling Ning recognized as a member of the Youth League. Now the girl rose.

" I say that Mr. Lu is '*ch'in mei*' — loves America — because he used to go over to Miss Graham's and eat foreign food lots of times, whenever she'd ask him." She giggled self-consciously and sat down.

"Yes," another girl popped up to say, "and in his room he has the picture of an American, a young man, and he says — he himself says — it's his 'pen pal,' and that means a friend you write letters to. And Mr. Lu himself said he'd written to that American for six years, ever since the American soldiers left after the Japanese surrender. The young man was an American soldier out here, and he used to give Mr. Lu presents. Mr. Lu told us himself. That shows he loves America. He would tear up the picture if he didn't."

Ling Ning saw that Mr. Yang had written twice on his pad, "Relevant."

The next speaker was a Shansi girl. She started out, in fairly good Peking Mandarin, to say that everybody else was willing to go to Korea — that only Mr. Lu wouldn't go, and that that showed how much he lacked patriotism. The longer she talked, the more she lapsed into her Shansi accent, until all Ling Ning could tell from what she was saying was that it was a hothearted patriotic speech, with a "love country" and an "American imperialism" in every sentence. The child talked on and on, until the girls themselves began to be restless. Ling Ning looked at Mr. Yang's pad. He had written, "Relevant, but not true."

When the girl finally finished, Principal Wang said: "I'm afraid we didn't all get that. What about it, Mr. Lu, did you understand her criticism?"

Mr. Lu's eyes sparkled in a smile. "You forget that I'm from Shansi myself. It's the accent of my childhood."

"Suppose you answer those three," the principal said.

Lu Min stood to speak. Ling Ning could see plainly that his knees were trembling. Her heart was full of pity and contrition. She had helped to bring him to this state.

He looked at his little notebook and said quietly: "I went

to Miss Graham's house and ate foreign-style food every time I could. I am guilty of that. I do not accept that as proof that I am on the American side in Korea. I do have the picture of a young American, and I have not torn it up. He is my friend, regardless of whether our two countries are enemies, until the People's Government shall announce that such personal friendships are disloyal. Whenever that happens, I shall give him up. I do not agree that everybody but Mr. Lu is going to Korea. What I said was that my not going did not prove that I love America any more than Miss Pu's not going proves that she loves America. I'm willing to stand by that statement." He sat down.

Empress was on her feet. "There! That's the way he talks. He's been doing that for two days with the Student Union. How can anybody argue with that?" She waved a disgusted hand in the direction of the platform.

"I criticize Mr. Lu because he won't grade our papers," the next girl said. Ling Ning had seen her pointed out as a leading Christian student, and was surprised that she should join the forces against Lu Min. Then honesty reminded her that in Lu Min's eyes she herself was in the same class with this girl. She must not forget that he still did not know that she regretted so bitterly having accused him of telling her secrets. The girl was going on with a long complaint that Mr. Lu had written the comment that her paper was so mixed up she would have to straighten it out before he could make any corrections. "What kind of way is that for a teacher to help a student?" She talked at length, complaining that he had corrected everybody else's paper but had refused to correct hers, even when she carried it back to him.

"That's right," another girl piped up. "He won't answer our questions in class. We asked him whether the world was created by God or by work, and everybody knows the answer and it wouldn't take him a minute, but do you know what he said? He said it wasn't in the lesson and we had more than we could manage already without taking that up! He said that because our class met only twice a week we had to finish one lesson in the book every time, and any outside questions would have to be asked and answered outside of the class hour. What kind of teacher's that? Won't answer the pupils' questions! " She sat down with a pout.

" He likes some people! " another girl was prompt to add. " And you know who – Little Sister. He gave her part of her tuition money."

" And Miss Ling gave her part and acted like she didn't know anything about it when we asked her."

Ling Ning felt her cheeks getting red.

" And he said she got first in the race! " a rather bashful girl offered as her whole contribution.

" So did Miss Ling! "

" And she wouldn't let Tientsin and Little Sister sign up for Korea." Three girls were speaking almost at once.

The principal interrupted what was approaching confusion. " Leave Miss Ling till later! Miss Ling is not to be included in the criticism of Mr. Lu. And I take this opportunity to call the attention of those girls in the back of the room to the fact that this is neither the time nor the place to be eating peanuts."

" Well, what I have to say hasn't anything to do with Miss Ling," a girl began, rolling her eyes. " Did you see Mr. Lu helping Little Sister up the bank the day we went out to the country? I wonder why he helped Little Sister! " She acted as though there were something more she could say if she chose.

The oldest mathematics teacher stood up in his place. " I'll answer that one. Mr. Lu needn't bother." He grasped his right shoulder with his left hand. " It aches yet from the twenty or more I pulled up. Mr. Yang and Mr. Chen and Mr. Lu there, being younger, each pulled up twice as many. If Little Sister was among them, I'll guarantee he didn't know it."

The principal was not the only one who was smiling. " I think you needn't answer any of those," he said in a low tone to Lu Min. Ling Ning looked at Mr. Yang's pad. There were three entries of: " Irrelevant."

"He studied English and looks at American picture magazines," offered a little girl beside one of the Boys' School teachers.

Miss Pu stood up. A rustle of interest ran over the room. Ling Ning looked at Lu Min. He looked even sicker than before, but his eyes were clear and steady.

" Fundamentally Mr. Lu is pro-American along with his religion," she said. " He has an American religion, and he won't give it up. Then how can you expect him not to be pro-American in other things? " She talked longer than any of the girls had done, including the little girl from Shansi, but all her remarks would have boiled down into her three opening sentences.

When she had finished, the principal again interrupted, refusing to recognize several girls who had jumped to their feet. " I shall ask you not to discuss religion. That means you too, Mr. Lu. You know a great deal more about it than Miss Pu does, and could doubtless go on indefinitely." He gave Lu Min one of his friendly smiles, and then, turning toward Miss Pu, continued: " Miss Pu is not an authority on this subject. It was not until we discussed the Fu Jen affair that she learned that Roman Catholics and Protestants worship the same God and follow the same Jesus." He raised his eyebrows in question, and she reluctantly nodded.

Then he turned to the girls. " In what she has just said she seemed to think Christianity was an American religion. Chinese Christians take pride in the fact that Jesus was a fellow Asiatic. Moreover, Christianity is now one of the Chinese religions. Our People's Government has given it that status by appointing five delegates to represent Christians at the People's Consultative Conference. In view of that fact, no one can say Christianity is any more an American religion than it is a Chinese religion. It is found in every country. What led Miss Pu astray is that in Wangshan, Christianity has been propagated by Americans. The religion is not American, but the institutions it has fostered, like these schools and the hospital, are heavily tainted with American patterns. And it is altogether possible that Mr. Lu, having been trained in such schools, has taken on a friendliness to American ways. Such a criticism would be to the point if you think it applies. However, I'll ask you not to bring religion into our discussion."

Miss Pu was on her feet at once. " The Americans claim they've been awfully nice to us to give us all these buildings and things. Of course we thank them. But if they hadn't started these schools, by now we'd have had just as good or better ones." She had had the last word, but she had not taken advantage of the opportunity the principal had given her to accuse Lu Min of being pro-American through his education.

When she sat down, half a dozen girls wanted to speak. The principal chose them, one after the other, and listened courteously to each. Most of them said only a sentence or two about whatever they disliked in Lu Min. Mr. Yang's little pad was full of " irrelevant." After several had spoken, the principal always called Lu Min, and the latter always answered very briefy, upholding his original position.

After one such answer, a very pert first-year girl jumped up and called out quite loudly, as though she was afraid she wouldn't be heard: "He's a smart man. He could answer lots better than that if he wanted to. I move we have him do it over."

Nobody paid any attention to her. There were too many other girls wanting to speak.

Ling Ning grew tired of their chatter. She watched Lu Min. He really was exhausted, though his mind was alert, intensely so. How she pitied him! As before, her pity was full of self-reproach. "I could pray for him," she thought.

Sometimes she did pray to the God Lu Min had made reasonable and real to her. He had said that the great benign creative power was available to help anyone who was working in harmony with Him, if the person was receptive to his power. When she prayed, she never said much, asking in simple words for what she wanted. So she looked at Lu Min with the pity she felt and said in her heart, "Heavenly Father, help him now when he needs it so." She could not see that it made any difference to Lu Min, but she believed it would.

At ten o'clock there was a short recess. Ling Ning was glad for the chance to reconnoiter. Yes, the man was in the office, busily writing at his desk. That meant that when she came to get the papers stamped, she would find the office open. The recess was very brief. Going back to the assembly hall, she met Tientsin. The girl stopped nervously, as though to tell some secret.

"It's all right," Ling Ning said before the girl could speak. She was sure it was unwise to let Tientsin tell her anything at all, and accompanied her assurance with as confident a smile as she could manage.

They were soon back in the meeting, and at once the man

from the educational department started his speech. As soon as Ling Ning saw him get up, she realized how foolish she had been to come back. Why had she not gone, while she was free outside, and hidden in Granny Mi's room, or in her own room, of which Granny Mi now had the key? How could she have been so stupid? This man might talk for two hours, and it would be impossible to get out until he had finished. Ling Ning did not hear a word he said — she was so frantic.

He did talk on and on. She wished she had some pepper so she could sneeze her way out of this. The thought put another idea into her head. Couldn't she pretend to some other kind of sickness, nosebleed or something? She watched the clock. At eleven the man was giving no evidence that he was approaching the end.

She looked at Lu Min to nerve herself for what she must do. Again she was touched by his patient endurance. "I said I'd do it for him," she said to herself, and began to cough with all her might. As soon as it might seem that she couldn't stop, she ran for the door, coughing all the way. Let them make what they could out of that!

Chapter 10

No one was in the courtyard. She ran into the deserted teachers' room, went to her desk, and quickly made sure everything was as she wanted it: the review work arranged so neatly that whoever gave her examinations would have the minimum of trouble. Her body was trembling with excitement. This was the crucial time. She prayed, "Heavenly Father, help me now," and went into the office.

Only the office secretary was there, writing intently at his desk. He looked up, with the harassed look of one interrupted at pressing work. "These Government reports have to be in at twelve," he said.

"Then I'll talk fast. I'm going to Peking on the bus today. I don't want anybody to know it till I'm gone, with the girls so excited — "

He nodded impatiently.

"Don't tell even Principal Wang. I'll leave a letter for him. I'd like to borrow half a month's salary." He was already moving toward the safe. She had been sure other teachers did it, and it was long past the fifteenth. "And I need the proper school seal to put on my application to the police for residence transfer. You won't need to know why I borrowed the money, and if they ask about the seal, put the blame on me — like, you went to the toilet or something for a few minutes and I could have used it while you were away." He certainly would be asked, not about hers, perhaps, but about Lu Min's. He had better have his story ready. "I'll stamp it. You don't need to help. I'm sorry to have bothered you this much, when you're so rushed."

He was already back at his copying before she had finished her sentence.

Ling Ning stood with her back to him and hurriedly stamped the eight sheets. She put the seal back on his desk and with a hurried "Thank you," went out the door.

Again no one was in the court. Her soft cloth shoes made no noise on the pavement. She almost ran. She must not be caught now!

She was barely out of sight around the corner, when she heard the door of the assembly room open, and the voices of Miss Pu and the man from the education bureau. Evidently he was not staying through the meeting. How nearly they had come to seeing her! And what could she have said?

She ran as fast as she could through court after court to her own. She had nothing to stop for. Already Granny Mi had her note to give the principal after the bus left. With only a glance toward her room, she opened the lock on the little gate, went out, and pulled it shut.

She was out! With the papers stamped!

There was no time for loitering in self-congratulation. She hurried along the familiar little alley, and when she saw Timmy Tan waiting with the bicycles, began to run again.

He did not need to ask her whether she had succeeded. "Now for the police office!" he said, and they were off.

The gate of the old yamen was familiar territory, but the front offices held no nostalgic memories.

"This fellow in here is pretty smart," Timmy warned

her. " We must be careful not to make a slip. I don't think he knows either Lu Min or me by sight, so we'll not tell him anything, and if he thinks, because I use his seal, that I'm Lu Min in person, don't correct him. It's perfectly legal to get a residence transfer for someone else. I just don't want to call the attention of this police officer to either of you. You're not out of town yet."

But in the registration office a girl was in charge. She was pleasant and chatty, and quick, but a little diffident. " Comrade Liu has just gone to a meeting, and I hope nobody wants anything I don't know how to do."

They assured her they wanted only residential transfers, and she said that was one thing she was sure she knew about. As Timmy Tan had foreseen, she took for granted he was Mr. Lu. On the blanks they gave Ling Ning's street number in Peking as the place to which they were moving, and research in chemistry and bacteriology as their future occupations. The girl failed to ask the one question Ling Ning was afraid of: whether her permanent transfer of residence meant she had received permission from the Government education department to sever her connection with the Wangshan Girls' School. Whatever might be the reaction of the men in the bureau when they heard she was gone, the girl cheerfully gave her a legal transfer of residence. And what was more important, as soon as they had the paper she wrote for Lu Min, there was no longer any necessity for his getting into trouble with the Peking police over the lack of one.

With genuine gratitude, Ling Ning and Timmy Tan thanked her and hurried from the building, hardly believing their good fortune.

" You're not out of town yet, and neither is Lu Min, but all's well so far, and here's hoping," Timmy muttered as they got on their wheels to return to the hospital. Timmy stayed with her there in the rear gatehouse, where they made a quick lunch of sesame cakes and fruit which the gatekeeper bought for them from one of the many food venders on the big street. They planned to wait out of sight until time to go to the bus.

There Nurse Sun found them. Just before the clinic closed at twelve, four schoolgirls had rushed in panting, looking for Miss Ling. They reported that she had left the criticism meeting early, and they had supposed she had gone to the clinic. When asked why they were looking for her, one said they " had business " with her, but one of the others giggled and said they were anxious about her health. They had been so persistent in declaring that Nurse Sun had Miss Ling hidden in her room, that she had finally led them there and showed them it was empty, being all the time in a state of terror for fear Ling Ning might walk in while she was talking to them.

Timmy Tan looked grave. " We've got to get you on today's bus whether Lu Min catches it or not. We may have our hands full if the girls think you're up to something. If you're once on the bus — "

" I have an idea! " Nurse Sun exclaimed. " We've got a patient leaving today, that Old Man Chang who goes about an hour's ride from here. He really isn't well enough to travel alone, and they were supposed to come for him, but they've sent word to put him on the bus and they'll guarantee to meet him. They take the responsibility, so we're sending him. You can be his daughter."

They dressed her in one of her own long garments over her padded uniform. Not a bit of the uniform showed from under the dark old-fashioned figured silk, but she looked so fat with so many clothes on that she set them laughing. Her hair was unbraided and made into a tight knot. Over her nose and mouth she wore a mask, such as had become so popular for street wear in the winter time, ever since the Japanese occupation. Nurse Sun found an old pair of sunglasses, and to top it all, covered her head completely with a bright green chiffon veil.

"Not even Lu Min will know you!" Timmy Tan declared, delightedly.

At the mention of his name a shadow fell on them all. What might Lu Min be enduring now? Suppose, as was very likely, Pirate got no chance to tell him that Timmy Tan had taken his things for safekeeping, and he thought he had lost them all! And how he would worry when he was forced to leave without a residence transfer! He knew nothing of the good fortune that was following his friends working on his behalf. For him days of childish persecutions were being followed by one disappointment after another. And if he remembered Ling Ning –

The orderly who pushed the wheel chair the few steps from the hospital to the bus station got no hint that the solicitous "Miss Chang" who, he supposed, had come for her father was anything other than she appeared to be. The little party went early to the bus station and found that so far only a few passengers had collected for the trip to Peking. When the bus came in, the driver that day proved to be a great friend of Timmy Tan, who had a way of making friends of everybody he met. Since the day was so blustery, the driver allowed those who were waiting to get in and arrange themselves as comfortably as they could. He chose for Old Man Chang the seat behind his own, which he claimed rode more comfortably than the others, and having been taken to one side for a little talk by Timmy Tan, came back apparently in great good humor.

" I don't like girl students," he muttered to Ling Ning, and she knew she had an ally.

Timmy had seen to all the baggage, both Ling Ning's and Lu Min's. He had brought it from the hospital and now the big pieces were roped securely on the roof of the bus. All Ling Ning's little things were inside flour sacks tied into the most nondescript of the sort of bundles Chinese travel with. In her hands she carried only Nurse Sun's thermos bottle, of a different shade of bright green from her veil, and a small parcel or two that belonged to Old Man Chang. Nothing about her could possibly remind a girl student of their teacher, Miss Ling.

For herself she felt now comparatively confident. But there was still no sign of Lu Min. A moment before Timmy Tan had grinned at her from the open door of the bus and said: " I guess you're off all right. The bus driver has everything under control." Now he was standing by Nurse Sun and keeping a constant watch up the street. He too was nervous about Lu Min. Suppose the girls decided to keep him there another day, or even more. Their will was the " will of the masses " and he would have to endure their treatment, whatever it was. He had looked so pale!

Ling Ning could see up the street too, and there was no Lu Min in sight. Suddenly she thought: " Why don't I pray for him? He's surely too flustered to pray for himself," and, following her recently acquired habit, she prayed as simply as she always did, " Heavenly Father, help Lu Min now."

The bus driver, who had been in the station, came and got on. " We've five minutes more," he said in a low tone that only Ling Ning sitting just behind him heard. " And if I have to, I'll wait a minute or two longer for him."

But it was not going to be necessary. Around the corner

by the hospital came a crowd of girls, and in the midst of them, carrying on his shoulder a bundle of bedding, was the hapless Lu Min. The girls' shrill voices could be heard at that distance in a medley of shouts. They came rushing directly toward the bus, and as they came nearer, occasionally one of their sentences would be clear enough to be understood. They were so wrought up that they were yelling to give vent to their feelings.

"I told you I don't like 'em," the driver muttered again. "They don't know what a sight they're making of themselves."

The students permitted the mechanic who traveled with the bus to put Lu Min's bedding on the roof with the other baggage, since there was no possibility of his taking it inside, but they yelled that he was not to buy a ticket.

"Let him pay double on the bus for being without one."

Timmy Tan pushed his way through the girls, ignoring the black looks they gave him, and walked by Lu Min to the door of the bus.

Meanwhile, Ling Ning heard a shrill voice: "There's Nurse Sun. What did I tell you? She probably has Miss Ling in the bus station ready to put her on at the last minute. Don't let Miss Ling on. We mustn't let her get away. If she comes out, pack a tight circle around her. We can handle her."

The girls were watching the door of the bus station. One ran and looked in, but came back, shaking her head. Several others ran around the bus looking through the windows to check on the passengers. They too were unsuccessful. Ling Ning would not be traveling with an old man, nor would she have been dressed in those clothes. It was no wonder they failed to recognize her.

Timmy Tan talked to Lu Min in English, which he knew

the girls would not understand. " It'll come out all right in the end, Lu Min. Before ever you get to Peking, things will begin to look different. I'm coming down next week myself, and I'll look you up."

" I'll let you know where I am," Lu Min answered.

" I'll find you all right. The bus driver has your ticket and your seal and a letter in which I reported on some things I wanted to tell you. I couldn't be sure I'd get even a word with you. If you hadn't got here, I'd have taken them back the last minute, but I thought it was better not to plan to hand you anything for fear some of the girls might come along. Let 'em think they succeeded in everything." He put all his loyalty into the smile he gave Lu Min, who was plainly on the verge of breaking down.

The engine started, and Timmy gave Ling Ning a farewell grin and a " Happing Landings! " and pushed back from the door.

Ling Ning heard someone cry out with sadistic delight, " Miss Ling didn't get here! "

The girls were getting closer, and now they began to revile Lu Min. They started with " Lover of America," " Coward," " Afraid to fight," but soon added " Running dog," " Rotten turtle egg! " and all the other bad words they knew. Those nearest began to kick at his legs, but he hopped on the bus well out of their reach. Denied that satisfaction, they spit at the bus while the door was closing and it was getting under way. A few minutes left them far behind.

Through the screen of her veil Ling Ning watched Lu Min. The bus was not crowded. Having taken from the driver the small packet Timmy Tan had left for him, Lu Min sat down three seats behind her on the other side of the bus. She could see him well in the driver's mirror, and no scenery could have been interesting enough to distract her. She had for days wanted a chance to talk to him, to apologize to him, to become friends again. Now that she could do it, she decided to wait until Old Man Chang had been turned over to his relatives, and Lu Min could have the seat beside her. She would continue to play the daughter a little while longer.

Lu Min sat staring ahead of him, as if he had come to the end of the way. In the morning his body had appeared utterly exhausted, but his eyes had been keen. Now even his eyes were heavy with weariness.

After a long time Lu Min remembered that his hand held a message from Timmy Tan. Slowly he opened the letter. Ling Ning could tell what he was reading, because a look of incredulity came over his face, and he hastily opened the other folded paper. His relief when he saw the residence transfer made up for what worry it had been to her to get it. He no longer faced trouble with the Peking police; he was out of the trap the girls had laid for him. Eagerly he turned back to the letter. She could tell when he read that she would be on the bus with him. He sat up straighter, and eagerly began to look over the other passengers, till now unheeded.

She had wondered if he would ever speak to her again. She needed no other assurance than the look of happiness on his face as he searched for her. Not finding her, he looked more slowly. This time he stood up to do it. Again failing to see her, he returned to the letter and read it through to the end.

Ling Ning's heart reproached her for his disappointment, but at the same time it was light with anticipation. As Timmy had promised, everything was going to be all right.

The bus had long since left the good Wangshan County road which she thought of as a monument to her uncle.

Now they bumped along through a bleak countryside. To Ling Ning the blustery day seemed no longer dreary. She had quite forgot the old man beside her until she heard his feeble voice saying, "We're nearly there." Looking ahead she saw a small walled town. There was nothing to do in preparation. The old man's few possessions were right at hand.

At the stop, as soon as the door was open, his relatives greeted him. Though Ling Ning had done nothing for him, he bowed and thanked her with stately old-time courtesy.

Ling Ning moved over into his seat beside the window, and jerked off veil, glasses, and mask. She turned to invite Lu Min to join her, her eyes dancing. He was looking out the window. She had been for a long time too warm with the long coat over her padded uniform. Disregarding the lurching of the bus, she stood in the aisle and took off the coat. This caught the attention of everybody in the bus. Lu Min jumped up with a delighted, "Ling Ning!"

With him sitting beside her and looking so happy, she did not find it hard to offer him her apology. And it gladdened her to hear him laugh.

"Miss Pu was really puffed up over that! We hadn't even been talking about you. She'd been threatening me with accusations by the Youth League. But I suppose when you walked in she saw her chance. She's smart!"

"Mr. Yang told me what a fool I'd been to believe her. And then I was afraid you'd never forgive me. Nurse Sun said you would because you believe in forgiving, and anyway — " She faltered, and felt herself blushing.

"Anyway what?"

She hadn't planned to tell him the reason Nurse Sun had given, but the look she gave him was just as effective.

There was no end to the things they had to tell each other

and there was no system in the telling. At length he asked her why she left the criticism meeting. " Don't you think I did it cleverly? " she asked after she had given him his answer.

He roared with laughter. " I was sure at the time it was faked. I haven't forgotten about the pepper."

" So you did know I was there. You never once looked at me."

" You looked at me often, and I could feel your sympathy. I thought you must have figured out that Miss Pu had fooled you, and that I hadn't told your secret."

" Then why didn't you look at me? "

" Not with all those sharp eyes on me! Just before you left, I was feeling nearly at the end of my strength. I'd been with the Student Union for hours and hours. I had to pay such close attention that it was very hard."

Ling Ning was glad to see that he was recovering from the tension of those endless questionings.

" Just before you left — I could see you out of the corner of my eye — you looked at me with the deepest kindliness, as if you were trying to give me courage. At once I could feel myself change. I was adequate for as many hours as they wanted to keep it up."

" I was praying for you."

Lu Min was surprised. " You were praying for me! I didn't know you prayed."

" Don't you remember explaining to me how prayer could be efficacious if it was the act of putting a person into harmony with God's will? I was sure you were in harmony, but I was afraid you needed strength, and that's what I asked for you." She was like a child in her simplicity. " I've done it before for myself when I faced something I couldn't master alone. You told me — "

"Yes, Ling Ning, I told you," he said — and added reverently, "'I have not found so great faith, no, not in Israel.'"

She wasn't sure what he meant. It sounded as though it might be a quotation. Neither was she surprised that her prayer had helped. That was what she had asked — help. At that moment her foot touched the thermos bottle sitting on the floor near the wall, and reminded her of what she had planned to do the minute she finished apologizing.

"Your lunch!" She picked up the bottle, and dragged one of her bundles from under the seat. "What would Nurse Sun think of me for keeping you waiting so long! She was sure you'd get no proper meal, and sent you something."

"I had no lunch," Lu Min admitted. "The girls went off to eat, but left somebody to watch me for fear I'd get away. Funny little people! So hothearted they had to stay up all night doing what could have gone undone!"

"You don't sound angry at them at all. The little fiends!"

"I'll forgive them sooner or later. Why not sooner, and be done with it? They're sadly misled. They think that abusing a person like me is a patriotic act, practically equivalent to going to Korea to fight. They know so little! But they're young yet." He ate one of the big soft balls of steamed bread from Nurse Sun's pasteboard box.

"She sent bread and hard-boiled eggs and tea," Ling Ning explained. "She was sorry the bread would be cold, but the tea's hot. She thought that if, as we suspected, you'd been half-starved, these would be better than oily food like *shao ping*. You can fill up at supper."

"It's perfect," Lu Min assured her, "and wonderfully thoughtful of you."

"Of Nurse Sun," she corrected. "Now while you eat, I'll tell you how Timmy and I got the residence transfers."

She told him the details. There was plenty of time, and it was all full of interest to him. "When we filled in the applications, we couldn't ask you what you wanted to put down. We put down what we thought best."

"I'm sure it will be satisfactory. Like what, for instance?"

"Well, an address. Where were you planning to go?"

"I don't know; I've been wondering."

"For this one night at least, you have no choice. You have to go where we said, and register with the local police office. We must do it as soon as we get there, even though it's after dark."

"And where do I go?"

"We put down my house. I know Mother has room for a guest, and I don't know where else would be so easy. I hope you don't mind. It's a good thing you forgave me. If you hadn't, it would have been rather awkward to introduce you to my mother." She was giggling.

"It's more than kind of you, but I don't feel so sure as you do that your mother is going to welcome unexpected company."

"You don't know my mother as well as I do. She'll like it. The other thing was 'future occupation.'"

"What did you put down for that?"

"For both of us, 'graduate research,' you in bacteriology and me in chemistry. What made me think of it was that I was asked to stay at Yenching to work in the graduate school, and I thought that if they'd have taken me, they'd be even happier to get you. I let the girl think they were just about waiting for us to get there. They have been, ever since summer, but they didn't know it." She giggled again.

"That's not a bad idea. I love to teach, but I don't seem to have made much of a success. Some graduate work would be all right for a while."

"Timmy said it would be easier to get excused from a teaching job if we were going some place to study than if we just wanted to quit. If we change our minds later, it's not likely that they'll follow us up to check on it."

At towns along the way the bus picked up passengers for Peking and was now crowded. The sun came out briefly and then set. The short winter day ended long before they arrived in Peking. Lu Min and Ling Ning talked on and on, as if they would never be able to make up for the days they had lost.

But at length they were traveling through the Peking suburbs, then through the great city gate, and through the streets. People got off at every stop. Lu Min and Ling Ning went all the way to the Tan Pailou in the East City. When they alighted, the bus driver got out too, ostensibly to help get their baggage down from the roof of the bus.

"Good-by, folks," he said. "I've never had, and I never hope to have, a more interesting ride down from Wangshan. Good luck to the two of you."

Chapter 11

Nothing in Lu Min's experience had prepared him for Ling Ning's mother, nor the house in which she lived. As a homeless boy in a Christian boarding school, he had sometimes been invited to the pastor's home, or to spend a few days with a schoolmate. The houses were simple and furnished as simply as the school dormitories. The mothers in these homes were unassuming Christian women, most of whom, being able to read, were therefore better educated than their neighbors, but for all that, thoroughly unsophisticated. The Bible women he had known were like country housewives. In high school and university he had met educated women teachers and fellow students, but often they too were of the great farmer class. Even Ling Ning herself, though she was so like her mother, had not prepared him for an older woman who personified China's ancient culture.

Her home, he thought, was worthy of her. Lu Min could perceive as soon as he entered that it was rich with carved partitions and furniture, the loveliest of the old, combined with Peking rugs and comfortable chairs, the most luxurious of the new.

Taken by surprise, Mrs. Ling showed no perturbation, welcomed Lu Min most graciously, and accepted pleasantly Ling Ning's plan that the trip to the police station should be made at once.

" And then you'll want some supper," she said.

" We know it's long past the time, but we are hungry," Ling Ning admitted. " Anything will be all right, if it's hot. Can't you get some cabbage soup or something from the restaurant? There isn't time to make it here, and anyway we need food and can leave the formalities till tomorrow. We won't be long."

Half an hour later they were back, and Lu Min was shown through a door on one side into a three-room building in a tiny court, quite shut off from the main yard.

" This was the master's study," the old gateman said. " Now it is used for guests. I hope you'll find it comfortable. It's still pretty cold, with the fire just lighted, but you're to come over to the living room when you're ready."

Lu Min thought he would have no trouble being comfortable in these rooms. He had never lived in any place so abundantly furnished with everything he could want. When he left Wangshan, he had wondered what sort of inn he could find. He appreciated all the more Ling Ning's thoughtfulness in inviting him here.

A few minutes later, approaching the living room door, he heard Ling Ning's excited voice and knew that she was relating the latest Wangshan events. Inside, he found the table set and a boy from the restaurant waiting to serve supper.

" You see, I took my daughter's good advice, and here's hot food and not much ceremony." Mrs. Ling sat down with them and saw to it that they had all they could eat of the four dishes she had ordered: spinach and eggs, mushrooms with chicken, water chestnuts, and cabbage soup, rice, and steamed bread.

When he could eat no more, Lu Min looked at Ling Ning and asked, " Can you remember as long as twelve hours ago? "

" I think someone was asking you why you pulled Little Sister up the bank," she answered.

" Ling Ning has told me a little of what you have been doing," Mrs. Ling said. " My suggestion is that you do now what you would if you were staying at an inn — go and sleep a long night through. We'll have breakfast at nine. It's Christmas Sunday, and I think we'd all like to go to church."

" To church! " Ling Ning repeated, surprised.

" I wrote you that your uncle said he was sorry he hadn't helped any of us to be Christians, but I didn't write that I've been studying Christianity and finding it unexpectedly satisfying. I go to church, but there is a great deal I don't understand. The service is planned for people who know so much more about it than I do. What has given me comfort is the New Testament my brother once gave me. I've been reading the Gospels and memorizing the words of Jesus. You may think that's odd when I know so little about Christianity."

" That's not so hard for a person who memorized the Four Books when she was a girl," Ling Ning put in.

" It's not so hard as the Four Books," Mrs. Ling admitted, " and much more full of meaning; at least I find it so. But I do need somebody to explain the things I don't understand."

" Lu Min will," Ling Ning offered promptly. " He knows all about it, and he's a good teacher too."

" I'll be glad to help in any way I can," Lu Min agreed.

Like the Ethiopian who called Philip into his chariot, Mrs. Ling welcomed Lu Min into her home. " I have so wanted to find someone. I little thought you were bringing me the fulfillment of that desire. We'll keep you here till all our questions are answered. You can stay, can't you? "

" Nothing could be nicer for the present, anyway, but I hardly have the face — "

" Do! " Ling Ning prompted.

" Most gratefully then, for a few days," Lu Min said at once. " And I'll really be less stupid after I've slept."

" No more talking till tomorrow! " Mrs. Ling ordered, and bade him good night.

At Wangshan, ever since the Liberation, the congregation had never exceeded fifty. At the big church in Peking which Mrs. Ling attended on Christmas Sunday, the auditorium was full of joyous worshipers. For Lu Min, the carols, the reading of the Christmas story, the prayers, the sermon, restored and revived his soul as the long night's sleep had revived his body. He had lost his job and had no promise of another. He had no assurance that the next situation he found might not bring a repetition of the difficulties at Wangshan. But he had friends and a stanch faith in God, and he thought, with the psalmist, " The Lord is on my side; I will not fear: what can man do unto me? "

Ling Ning was happy too. For her the service had the freshness of the unfamiliar. She easily fitted what she heard into the framework of the things Lu Min had taught her. The enlivening joy and the quiet confidence alike inspired her. The prayers, so much more wordy than anything she knew, expressed many things she had not thought of. The old carols, all new to her, sung with familiarity and delight, raised her spirits. Seated between her mother and Lu Min, she forgot the troubles of the past and savored to the full the joyous present.

Lu Min knew the minister and many of the people and exchanged greetings with his friends. Several of the older women spoke to Mrs. Ling, recognizing her as one who attended regularly. Ling Ning did not know the people, but could feel the warmth of their friendliness.

At dinner Lu Min remarked on the absence of young

people of high school age and younger. " Didn't you notice the choir? " he said. " There were twelve or thirteen, no one under twenty-five. That church used to have a choir of forty or fifty high school and college students. And there were no teen-agers in the congregation either."

"There were three times as many people there as usual," Mrs. Ling said. " Other Sundays they meet in the parish house. I've never seen anybody of the high school age."

" Their absence means a great deal to the future of the church," Lu Min commented.

"Tientsin said she could stay this last term at Wangshan 'by not going to church.' She didn't seem to suggest that she could give up her belief," Ling Ning said. " Maybe they believe, but stay away."

" That's right. There are many Christian young people who are just lying low. It's hard for anyone not to run with the crowd, and almost impossible for an adolescent. But they are missing the experiences that are a training for their adult Christian life."

" The sort of thing you had, and I hadn't," Mrs. Ling added.

" And they are getting a very different set of experiences," Lu Min went on. " The Government gives them management of ever so many things that used to be taken care of by older people. For instance, those youngsters we've just been dealing with at Wangshan! Time was when children might drive a teacher out of their school, but these drove me out of town, carrying the onus of the lack of a residence transfer. The method is a complete overturn from the day when adults would be arraigned by adults before a judge, and represented by a trained lawyer."

" I think the children are a bit drunk with their power," Ling Ning said.

" It's the most natural thing in the world. How many

times in history have revolutionists overthrown a corrupt government only to misuse the power they won! Our People's Government rightly denounces the selfishness and injustice of the Kuomintang, but already there is selfishness and injustice in China. We Christians say it is because, in order to do away with such sins, the heart must be changed; changing outward circumstances is not enough."

Evening brought another service — a pageant of the Christmas story, acted in pantomime, with a reader and choir to tell the story. Again, as in the morning, for Lu Min there was balm in the familiar, and for Ling Ning and her mother there was attractiveness in the unfamiliar. They walked home under the brilliant North China winter stars, full of the harmony and hope of Christmas.

There were no Christmas customs in the Ling home: no carols, no Christmas tree, no hanging of stockings or cooking of special dishes. It had never been a day different from any other day. But on this Christmas morning Mrs. Ling said, "Today we'll eat *mien t'iao* — noodles — to celebrate a Birthday." Then she brought out some bright red paper cutouts, with patterns of three Wise Men on camels following a star, and of a Mother and Baby. "These are what the Bible woman said we should put up for Christmas. Is it now about the right time to do it?"

"You could have done it a week or two ago if you'd wanted to," Lu Min answered, "but now's a good time, when Ling Ning and I are here to help."

Ling Ning thought Lu Min less talkative than usual and wondered what was on his mind. Something must be lacking and he was too polite to mention it. Then she knew!

"Christmas presents!" she cried. "We've forgotton one of the essentials."

"I didn't forget, but there hasn't been much opportunity

to make purchases," Lu Min said. "Anyway, Christmas gifts don't have to be things — articles; they can be anything that will make another happy. Sometimes people tell what they'd like. Do you think that's a good idea?"

"If you knew what you wanted," she answered. "I don't know what I want."

"Don't you?" Lu Min said gently, and then, looking at Mrs. Ling, said, "I do."

Mrs. Ling smiled. "Do you think maybe I can guess? Only it's not the style nowadays to say anything to the old folks about it."

"I'm not so up to the minute as all that," Lu Min told her.

"What riddles are you two talking?" Ling Ning demanded.

"Ling Ning, there's only one thing right now that I really want, and I've been afraid to ask ever since I saw all this." Lu Min looked about the comfortable room. "Here I am without a job. How can I dare ask you to marry me?"

It appeared, from the look she gave him, that the idea appealed to her.

"Will you?"

"Any day you say!"

There was no demonstration of affection between them. That is not the custom in China. They gave each other a long, understanding look, in which at last they could free the tenderness they felt.

"You have known me such a short time!" Lu Min said to Mrs. Ling.

"I've heard considerable about you," she answered, smiling. "As I remember, the first letter from Wangshan started the singing of your praises."

Ling Ning blushed. "After all, he was wonderful to me. He was like a big brother, or maybe —"

"No, not a big brother," Lu Min said. "I had a different idea long ago."

"This is the best kind of Christmas present," Mrs. Ling remarked. "Lu Min gets the wife he wants. Ning gets the husband she wants. And I get a son. I'm sure I'm going to like that very much. I've wanted one for many years."

"You forgot to mention that I get not only a lovely wife, but a beautiful mother," Lu Min said. "I barely remember my own. I too am sure I'm going to like it."

There was a new excitement in all their talk of plans for the future. They would have a small wedding soon — very soon — why wait? They might even have it when Timmy Tan made his promised visit to Peking. They would look up the possibilities of graduate work.

"We're not too poor," Mrs. Ling said. "Go ahead and plan what will make you most useful. You may find that your contribution as scientists will be acceptable to our New China. The teaching you did was, in any case, one step in your growing up."

"It didn't hurt me to go through all those experiences at Wangshan," Lu Min agreed. "As you say, I'm more adult and ready for life. And I'm surely a stronger Christian on account of them."

"I wouldn't be a Christian at all if you hadn't been there and shown me what it means," Ling Ning said.

"Through those days I thought of myself as a rock in the midst of stormy waves. It is my part to stand fast and let the waves wash over me without dislodging me, and if they wash me cleaner, that's all the better. I've chosen a new name for myself — something to live up to — Peter. It means 'a rock.'"

"Like the Peter Jesus talked to," Mrs. Ling added, pleased that she understood. "'I shall call thee Peter,' Jesus said, 'and on this rock I will build my church.'"